Breaking the Rules

Dow Jones

Published by Century Books, 2024.

This is a work of fiction. Similarities to real people, places, or events are entirely coincidental.

BREAKING THE RULES

First edition. November 2, 2024.

Copyright © 2024 Dow Jones.

ISBN: 979-8227735218

Written by Dow Jones.

Also by Dow Jones

Breaking the Rules
Love's Dividends

Chapter 1: Collision Course

The air was electric as the sun rose over the city, casting a warm glow on the iconic stadium. The roar of the crowd reverberated through the streets, anticipation palpable as fans adorned in their team colors poured in. It was match day, and the stakes had never been higher.

Match Day Preparations

In the home locker room, Lucas stood before a mirror, adjusting their kit with meticulous care. With tousled dark hair and piercing green eyes, they were a striking figure—fierce and determined. A promising talent in the Premier League, Lucas was known for their relentless energy on the pitch, darting through defenses with lightning speed. As they tied their cleats, their heart raced not just with adrenaline, but with the weight of expectation. Today was a chance to prove they could hold their own against the seasoned veterans of the league.

Across the hall in the opposing locker room, Jamie was the epitome of charisma and confidence. With a chiseled jaw and a casual charm, they embodied the role of the star player. Renowned for their silky footwork and strategic mind, Jamie was a master of playmaking, often dictating the tempo of the game with their effortless style. They leaned back against the wall, grinning at their teammates, the faintest hint of mischief in their eyes. While Lucas thrived on speed and tenacity, Jamie preferred finesse and flair, often drawing defenders in before delivering a perfectly weighted pass.

Contrasting Styles on the Pitch

As the players emerged from the tunnel, the atmosphere shifted. Cheers erupted from one side of the stands, a wave of blue and white flags flapping proudly, while the opposite end surged with a sea of red and gold, chanting the names of their heroes. The contrast between the two players was evident even before the match began. Lucas soaked in the raw energy of their supporters, the underdog fighting for recognition, while Jamie basked in the adulation, reveling in the spotlight that had become their second skin.

The whistle blew, and the game commenced. Lucas wasted no time, sprinting forward, evading tackles with agility. Their movements were a blur, pushing the ball ahead as they outpaced their opponents. Every time they touched the ball, the crowd erupted, chanting their name with fervor. On the opposite end, Jamie surveyed the field with a calm, calculated demeanor. They dribbled the ball with grace, weaving through defenders as if they were mere obstacles rather than opponents. A flick of the foot here, a subtle shift of weight there, and the ball danced at their command.

Fan Reactions and Rising Tensions

As the first half progressed, the match teetered on the edge of chaos. Lucas's relentless pursuit and bursts of speed began to frustrate Jamie, who was unaccustomed to being pressured like this. The fans mirrored the tension on the pitch; gasps echoed when Lucas intercepted a pass, and cheers erupted when Jamie executed a perfectly timed backheel to create space for their teammate.

With every tackle and every close call, the rivalry intensified. Each player's supporters shouted louder, creating a cacophony of noise that filled the stadium. But amidst the cheers and jeers, there was an undercurrent of something deeper—a mutual respect brewing beneath the surface of their fierce competition.

As the half-time whistle blew, both players retreated to their respective benches, hearts pounding and bodies glistening with sweat. They exchanged glances across the field, each one silently acknowledging the other's skill. It was just the beginning of a long, arduous journey that would lead them down an unexpected path.

Rivalry on the Field

As the second half kicked off, the tension escalated, with both teams fiercely battling for possession. The stakes were higher than ever—the championship title loomed, and every pass, every tackle mattered. Lucas, fueled by the cheers of their fans, launched into the game with renewed vigor. Their speed was their weapon, darting down the flank and leaving defenders in their wake.

On the other side, Jamie remained a commanding presence, orchestrating plays with an effortless elegance. With their eyes scanning the field, they positioned themselves strategically, ready to exploit any weaknesses. Jamie was more than just a player; they were a leader, motivating their teammates with confident shouts and quick instructions. Each time Lucas attempted to break through, Jamie was there, standing as an imposing wall, a living embodiment of the seasoned player's cunning.

Showcasing Skills

Midway through the second half, the game reached a fever pitch. Lucas received the ball at the edge of the penalty area, their heart racing as they faced a trio of defenders. With a swift feint and a change of direction, they maneuvered past one, then another, their footwork dazzling as they weaved through tight spaces. The crowd erupted into a chorus of cheers, their anticipation palpable as Lucas approached the goal.

Jamie, sensing the threat, sprinted back, determined to put a stop to the burgeoning momentum. As Lucas wound up for a shot, Jamie slid in, expertly timing their challenge, the two players colliding in a cacophony of cleats and muscle. The moment hung suspended in the air, as the referee paused, considering the outcome of the challenge.

A Heated Exchange

"Get off me, you showboat!" Lucas spat, frustration boiling over as they regained their footing. They glared at Jamie, whose expression was a mix of smug satisfaction and playful defiance.

"I'll take you down any day, kid," Jamie retorted, brushing dirt from their kit with a wry smile. "You might have the speed, but you'll need more than that to get past me."

"Speed is all I need! You're just a relic trying to hold on to your glory days," Lucas shot back, the heat of competition flaring between them.

The crowd was caught in a frenzy, the back-and-forth electrifying the atmosphere. Teammates on both sides sensed the rising tensions, whispering amongst themselves, caught between laughter and disbelief. It was a duel, a clash of egos, and the stakes had never felt higher.

With a swift motion, the referee finally blew the whistle, signaling a foul against Lucas. The decision sent ripples of disappointment through their fans, while the opposing supporters erupted in cheers. As Lucas stomped back to their position, Jamie shot them a knowing glance, the competitive spirit igniting something unspoken between them.

The Game Rages On

The intensity of the match surged as both players dug deep, pushing themselves beyond their limits. Each play became a battle not only for victory but for respect. Lucas's determination was palpable; they lunged for every ball, challenged every defender, igniting the fervor of the crowd. Jamie, meanwhile, showcased their ability to read the game, anticipating movements and strategically placing passes that left their opponents scrambling.

As the final minutes ticked away, the score remained tied, and the pressure mounted. Lucas and Jamie, locked in their rivalry, exchanged glances that spoke volumes—both were driven, both were hungry for victory. But beneath the competitive facade, a spark of intrigue lingered, a tantalizing hint of something more.

The whistle would blow soon, but for now, the game raged on, and neither player was willing to back down.

The Final Whistle

As the final whistle blew, a deafening silence fell over the stadium, quickly followed by an eruption of mixed reactions. The home team had lost, and the atmosphere turned electric with disbelief and disappointment. Lucas stood frozen for a moment, heart pounding in their chest as the realization sank in. They had fought hard, pushed their limits, yet the game was snatched away by a controversial call.

Jamie, on the other hand, reveled in the moment, exchanging high-fives with teammates and basking in the joy of victory. But as they caught sight of Lucas's desolate expression across the field, the exhilaration dimmed slightly. They couldn't ignore the look of frustration and anger etched across their rival's face.

Frustration and Blame

In the locker room, the mood was somber. Lucas slammed their locker shut, the sound echoing off the walls, frustration bubbling over. "That was a terrible call! We had that game in the bag!" they exclaimed, their voice tinged with rage.

Teammates shuffled awkwardly, unsure of how to respond, but Lucas didn't care. "We worked so hard for this! I can't believe the ref—"

"Sometimes, it's just the way it goes," one of the older players interjected, trying to diffuse the tension. But Lucas was having none of it, their emotions flaring.

"I get that, but we shouldn't have lost because of someone else's incompetence!" They paused, the weight of their words sinking in. Lucas felt the eyes of their teammates on them, but all they could think about was the bitter taste of defeat.

Across the hall, Jamie was reveling in the victory with their own teammates, but the jubilation felt hollow. They had fought hard for this win, yet seeing Lucas so upset tugged at something within. "They really gave it their all out there," Jamie mused aloud, eliciting nods from their teammates.

A Heated Confrontation

After the post-match debriefing, Lucas stormed into the hallway, still fuming. As they rounded a corner, they came face to face with Jamie. The air thickened with tension, each player radiating frustration.

"Nice job out there, showboat," Lucas snapped, the words sharper than intended. "I hope you're proud of winning a game that should've gone the other way."

Jamie raised an eyebrow, the playful demeanor evaporating. "What's your problem? I didn't make the call. We played better, that's all."

Lucas stepped closer, their anger boiling over. "You think you're so great just because you're in the spotlight. You don't care about anyone but yourself."

"That's rich coming from you," Jamie shot back, stepping forward as well, their faces inches apart. "You think running fast makes you a better player? It's about strategy, about reading the game, something you clearly don't understand."

Setting the Stage for Change

Their heated exchange echoed down the hallway, drawing curious glances from passing teammates. Both players were breathing heavily, the rivalry that had ignited on the field spilling over into personal territory. Yet, beneath the anger, there was a flicker of something else—a challenge that lingered, a recognition that they were both passionate about the game.

The standoff continued until Lucas, taking a deep breath, broke the silence. "Whatever. Enjoy your victory." With that, they turned sharply, storming away, leaving Jamie staring after them, conflicted.

As Lucas walked away, frustration began to give way to something more complex. They didn't want to admit it, but the intensity of their emotions—anger, rivalry, and maybe even admiration—was something they hadn't expected. Jamie watched them go, a sense of respect growing alongside the rivalry. They knew they'd face Lucas again, both on and off the pitch, and the next encounter would be anything but simple.

The game was over, but the real contest had just begun—a dance of rivalry, passion, and perhaps, the hint of something deeper.

Chapter 2: Unlikely Allies

The Charity Gala Announcement

The following week, the buzz of the Premier League continued to ripple through the media, but amidst the excitement of match reviews and player interviews, a different event was making headlines: a charity gala aimed at raising funds for underprivileged youth programs in the community. The event promised a star-studded lineup, but the headlines were dominated by one surprising announcement—Lucas and Jamie, rivals on the pitch, would be the headlining guests.

Lucas stared at the invitation in disbelief, a mix of irritation and dread washing over them. "There's no way I'm showing up to this," they muttered to themselves, tossing the glittering card onto the table.

However, the voice of their manager echoed in their head, reminding them of the importance of public relations. "You need to keep your profile up, especially after that match. This is a great opportunity," they'd said. So, with a reluctant sigh, Lucas pulled out their phone and texted their agent, confirming their attendance.

The Night of the Gala

On the night of the gala, the venue was lavishly decorated, with twinkling fairy lights draping the ceilings and elegant tables set with sparkling crystal centerpieces. Celebrities mingled, laughter and music filled the air, but Lucas felt a knot of anxiety in their stomach. They wore a tailored suit, the fabric sharp and crisp, but it felt constricting, much like the atmosphere surrounding the event.

As guests arrived, Jamie made their entrance, exuding charisma in a tailored ensemble that perfectly complemented their confident stride. The moment they stepped onto the red carpet, cameras flashed, and the crowd roared, drawn in by their magnetic presence. Jamie was in their element, waving to fans and posing for pictures, but their eyes darted around, searching for the one person they were obligated to interact with tonight.

When Lucas finally arrived, they felt the tension in the air shift. The moment they spotted Jamie, their heart raced—not with excitement, but with an unyielding urge to confront. As the two approached each other, the smiles plastered on their faces felt forced, the tension between them palpable.

Tense Initial Interactions

"Great to see you here," Jamie said, their tone light but eyes glinting with competitive fire.

"Yeah, well, not everyone gets to enjoy the limelight like you do," Lucas shot back, their voice edged with sarcasm. "Must be nice being the crowd favorite."

Jamie smirked, leaning against a nearby table. "And here I thought we were supposed to be raising money for a good cause. But I guess you'd rather sulk than play nice."

"I'm not sulking. I just don't think pretending to be friends is going to help anyone," Lucas replied, crossing their arms defensively.

As the charity representatives called for both players to come to the stage, the tension reached its peak. "Look," Jamie said quietly, just as they were about to be announced, "let's just get through this without tearing each other apart, okay?"

Lucas hesitated, feeling a flicker of uncertainty. They didn't want to agree, but they knew they had to keep up appearances. "Fine. But this doesn't mean I like you," they replied, their voice low enough that only Jamie could hear.

Public Appearance and Forced Camaraderie

As they stepped onto the stage together, the crowd erupted into applause. Jamie took the lead, effortlessly engaging with the audience, while Lucas forced a smile, feeling the weight of their irritation boil beneath the surface. The charity representatives introduced them, praising their involvement in the event, and the tension crackled in the air as they spoke about their experiences in football and the importance of giving back.

When it was time for questions from the audience, the first one directed at them was about their infamous rivalry. "How do you manage to work together despite being competitors?"

Lucas's instinct was to retort, but Jamie chimed in first, playing the diplomat. "We both want to make a difference in our community," they said smoothly, glancing at Lucas. "Even if we have different styles, we share a common goal tonight."

Lucas felt a flicker of irritation at Jamie's easy charm, but couldn't deny the truth in their words. When it was Lucas's turn to speak, they kept it simple. "We've had our differences, but this cause is bigger than us. It's about the kids."

The audience clapped, and as they exchanged glances, Lucas noticed a hint of understanding in Jamie's eyes, beneath the competitive facade. The evening continued with more forced camaraderie, photo ops, and mingling with guests.

As the night wore on, Lucas found themselves caught off-guard by the sincerity of some of Jamie's comments, the way they genuinely engaged with the children they met, bending down to speak to them, their laughter infectious. It was an unfamiliar side of their rival—one that challenged Lucas's perceptions, if only for a moment.

A Shift in Atmosphere

As the gala progressed, the initial tension between Lucas and Jamie began to dissipate, replaced by a cautious curiosity. After an engaging speech from the charity's founder, guests were encouraged to mingle and enjoy the evening's festivities. Lucas found themselves standing near the buffet, reluctantly filling their plate while stealing glances at Jamie, who was deep in conversation with a group of fans.

After a few moments, Jamie broke away, making their way toward Lucas. "What did you get?" they asked, eyeing the plate piled high with gourmet food.

"Just the usual—nothing fancy," Lucas replied, trying to sound nonchalant as they gestured to the array of dishes.

Jamie chuckled, a genuine sound that caught Lucas off guard. "Fancy isn't my thing either. I prefer a good burger over this gourmet stuff any day."

Lucas raised an eyebrow, surprised at the unexpected commonality. "Really? I thought you lived on kale and protein shakes," they teased, a small smile creeping onto their lips.

"Only during training camp," Jamie admitted, leaning against the table. "After a game, I'm all about the comfort food."

Revealing Their Stories

The conversation started to flow more naturally, and as the atmosphere softened, Lucas found themselves opening up. "I grew up in a small town where nobody really cared about football," they began. "I had to fight for every chance to play, you know? It was like, if you didn't have the right connections, you were stuck."

Jamie nodded, their expression thoughtful. "I can relate. My family wasn't exactly rolling in money either. I played for a local team, and my parents sacrificed a lot to get me to training. I remember running through the rain just to make it to practice."

"Seriously? Same here! I'd ride my bike for miles, sometimes in the pouring rain, just to get to the pitch," Lucas said, their eyes widening in surprise.

"It's like we were both on the same journey, just in different parts of the world," Jamie mused, a hint of admiration in their voice.

Finding Common Ground

The unexpected similarities sparked a newfound sense of respect. Lucas leaned in, intrigued. "So what was it that kept you going? Why not give up when things got tough?"

Jamie paused, contemplating. "Honestly? It was the dream of making it to the Premier League. I wanted to prove to everyone that I could do it, even when they said I couldn't." Their voice grew quieter, revealing a vulnerability. "And my dad. He always believed in me, even when I didn't believe in myself."

Lucas felt a lump form in their throat, struck by the raw honesty in Jamie's words. "My mom was the same. She worked multiple jobs, just so I could have a chance. I never wanted to let her down," they admitted, the weight of their past surfacing.

"Sounds like we both have a lot to prove," Jamie replied, their gaze steady. "Maybe that's why we push each other so hard on the field."

The connection grew, the rivalry fading into the background as they shared more anecdotes about their early struggles, setbacks, and the relentless drive that fueled their passion for football. They discovered mutual friends from their youth leagues, shared favorite training drills, and exchanged tales of embarrassing moments during their early careers.

A Shift in Dynamics

As the night wore on, their conversation deepened, revealing layers they had never considered about one another. The gala, once a chore, became an opportunity to understand each other, to break down the walls built by competition and ego.

"I have to admit, I didn't think you'd be so easy to talk to," Lucas said, a hint of amusement in their tone.

Jamie smirked, "And I didn't expect you to have a sense of humor beneath all that bravado."

The banter continued, laughter spilling between them as they found common ground, shifting their dynamic from rivals to unlikely allies. There was still an edge of competition, a spark that hinted at the fire of their rivalry, but beneath it lay an emerging friendship forged through shared experiences.

As they finished their meal, the lights dimmed further, signaling the start of the auction for the charity. Jamie turned to Lucas, a mischievous grin on their face. "Ready to team up for a good cause? Let's show them what we can do together."

Lucas smiled back, a mix of camaraderie and excitement bubbling within them. "Yeah, let's do it. But just remember, I'm still the faster one."

With that, they stepped forward together, united for a common purpose, the tension of rivalry transformed into the promise of collaboration. The night was far from over, and as they prepared to work together, both players felt a shift in their relationship—one that hinted at deeper connections beyond the football pitch.

Collaborating on the Initiative

As the gala transitioned into the charity auction, Lucas and Jamie found themselves partnered for the event's centerpiece: a live auction where guests could bid for a chance to join them for a day of training at their club. It was a unique opportunity to engage fans while raising significant funds for the charity.

"Alright, let's do this," Jamie said, enthusiasm evident in their voice as they surveyed the crowd. "We'll make it fun!"

Lucas nodded, a competitive spark igniting within them. "I hope you know how to sell this. I'm not losing to you on the pitch or in fundraising."

Jamie grinned, raising an eyebrow. "Challenge accepted. But let's keep it civil, shall we?"

With the audience gathered, they took turns leading the pitch, showcasing their banter and camaraderie. Lucas began with a playful tone, "You'll get a chance to train with the best player in the league. You know, the one everyone talks about," they gestured toward Jamie, who feigned humility.

"Ha! And you'll get to learn from someone who's pretty good, too," Jamie chimed in, the chemistry between them palpable as they exchanged glances, igniting a spark of excitement in the crowd.

Lightening the Mood

As they took turns discussing the training experience, their competitive nature transformed the presentation into a lively back-and-forth. They shared funny anecdotes about their time on the field, each story eliciting laughter from the audience.

"There was that one time I slipped while taking a penalty kick," Lucas recalled, trying to suppress a grin. "The ball rolled a few feet, and I still managed to score—against my own team's goalkeeper!"

Jamie burst out laughing, shaking their head. "That's a classic! But remember when you thought you could outrun me in that charity match? You ended up in the goalpost instead."

"Hey, that was an accident! I'm still claiming it as a tactical move," Lucas shot back, their laughter infectious. The energy in the room shifted; the initial tension they'd felt was replaced by a sense of ease and connection.

As they engaged with the audience, a sense of genuine camaraderie developed. They found themselves naturally bouncing ideas off each other, crafting playful jabs and compliments that flowed effortlessly, drawing the crowd into their dynamic.

A Growing Connection

With every passing moment, their chemistry deepened. As they rallied the crowd for higher bids, Jamie leaned closer, whispering jokes and making sly remarks that made Lucas laugh harder than they had anticipated.

"Do you think they're really interested in our training or just want to see us mess up?" Lucas asked, still chuckling.

"Probably both," Jamie replied, nudging Lucas with their shoulder. "But let's give them a show."

With the energy building, they began to improvise, weaving in playful challenges for the audience—like bidding to see who could do the most push-ups or juggle a ball for the longest time. Their banter was seamless, and for the first time, Lucas realized they genuinely enjoyed Jamie's company.

As the auction progressed, Lucas caught Jamie's eye, a moment of silent understanding passing between them. This wasn't just about raising money; it was about connecting with each other, proving that they could work together despite their differences.

The Successful Auction

When the bidding finally closed, the amount raised surpassed all expectations. The crowd erupted in applause, and Jamie turned to Lucas, a triumphant smile on their face. "We did it! Who knew we made such a good team?"

"Don't get used to it," Lucas replied, but their grin belied the competitive edge. "We're still rivals, remember?"

"Of course. But rivals can also be friends," Jamie said, their tone sincere. The shift in their relationship felt palpable, as if they had crossed an invisible line from adversaries to allies.

As the night drew to a close, Lucas and Jamie stood side by side, basking in the success of the evening. They were surrounded by laughter and chatter, but it was the connection they had built that felt most significant.

"Want to grab a drink and celebrate?" Jamie suggested, tilting their head toward the bar.

"Sure, but I'm ordering something stronger than a protein shake," Lucas replied, feeling a thrill of anticipation as they walked toward the bar together, their rivalry softened by a newfound understanding.

With each step, they realized they were no longer just players from opposing teams. They were two individuals forging a bond, one that was unexpected and exhilarating, hinting at the potential for something more.

Chapter 3: Secrets and Vulnerabilities

A Quiet Corner

After the gala's festivities, Lucas and Jamie stepped away from the bustling crowd, seeking a quieter space to unwind. The lively chatter and laughter faded into the background as they found a secluded corner of the bar, where dim lighting cast a warm glow over their faces.

"I can't believe we actually pulled that off," Lucas said, leaning back in their chair with a sigh of relief. "Who knew we made such a good team?"

"Right? It felt different this time," Jamie replied, their expression thoughtful. "Like we actually connected instead of just competing."

"Maybe we're not as different as we thought," Lucas mused, tapping their fingers on the table. The alcohol flowed, easing their nerves and allowing the earlier tension to dissolve. "But I bet there's more to you than just the flashy goals and press conferences."

Sharing Personal Struggles

Jamie chuckled softly, taking a sip of their drink. "You're not wrong there. Everyone sees the glory, but they don't see the struggles behind it. Sometimes, I feel like I'm just a pawn in the game, you know? There's so much pressure to always be at the top."

Lucas nodded, feeling a wave of understanding wash over them. "Yeah, I get that. It's like we have to be perfect all the time, or we'll let everyone down. I've had my share of struggles too—there were times I doubted whether I belonged in the Premier League at all."

"Seriously?" Jamie leaned in, intrigued. "What made you doubt yourself?"

"After a big match where I messed up, I felt like I was the joke of the team," Lucas confessed, their voice dropping to a whisper. "I just wanted to prove that I wasn't a fluke. It's exhausting, feeling like you have to fight for every scrap of recognition."

Jamie's eyes softened, recognizing the weight behind Lucas's words. "I know how that feels. I had a terrible season last year. My performance dipped, and it felt like the fans turned on me. I started second-guessing everything—my training, my choices... even my passion for the game."

Opening Up

A silence enveloped them, filled with the weight of shared experiences. Lucas took a deep breath, feeling the atmosphere shift as they continued to share. "Sometimes, I think people forget we're human. They only see the athlete—the persona. No one really talks about the fears and insecurities that come with it."

Jamie nodded in agreement, their expression sincere. "It's like we're expected to be invincible. But what happens when we stumble? It's hard to admit when you're struggling, especially in this industry."

"I've been working with a sports psychologist recently," Lucas admitted, surprising even themselves with the vulnerability of the statement. "It's helped a bit, but I still feel like I carry this weight. I wish I could just be myself without the constant scrutiny."

"That's brave of you," Jamie said, admiration evident in their voice. "I've considered it too, but I always thought it was a sign of weakness. Maybe it's time we stop pretending everything's okay."

Finding Strength in Vulnerability

As they continued to talk, the barriers between them began to dissolve. They shared stories about their families, the sacrifices their loved ones made, and how those experiences shaped their dreams. With each confession, the connection between them deepened, revealing vulnerabilities that were rarely shared in the public eye.

"Sometimes, I wish I could just escape it all," Lucas said, looking down at their drink. "Just play for the love of the game without all the pressures."

Jamie reached across the table, their hand brushing against Lucas's. "You're not alone in that. I think we all crave that escape, a chance to just be ourselves without the expectations."

Feeling the warmth of Jamie's touch, Lucas met their gaze, surprised by the depth of emotion behind their words. In that moment, they realized that beneath the rivalry and competition lay a profound connection that neither had anticipated.

"Thanks for sharing this with me," Lucas said, a smile breaking through the tension. "It's nice to talk about this stuff, especially with someone who gets it."

"Anytime," Jamie replied, their voice softening. "We're in this together, even if it doesn't feel like it sometimes."

As the night wore on, they continued to share their stories, the bond between them growing stronger with every confession. Laughter mingled with the weight of their struggles, each moment fostering a newfound understanding that transcended the football pitch.

A Promise for Tomorrow

Eventually, the bar began to empty, and the two players found themselves lingering in the soft glow of the dim lights. Lucas looked around, realizing how late it had gotten. "I should probably head back. Tomorrow is another match day, after all."

"Yeah, me too," Jamie replied, but there was a reluctance in their voice, a hesitation to break the connection they had formed that night.

"Maybe we could do this again sometime?" Lucas suggested, a hopeful note in their tone.

"I'd like that," Jamie said, their smile genuine. "Let's not wait for another charity event. We can grab a drink or hit the pitch for some practice."

With a shared understanding and a promise of more conversations to come, they stood up from the table, the camaraderie between them blooming into something deeper. As they walked out into the cool night air, Lucas felt a spark of excitement, knowing this was just the beginning of a journey that could change everything.

A Moment of Reflection

As they stepped out of the bar, the cool night air wrapped around them, refreshing and invigorating. Lucas paused, leaning against the brick wall of the building, the streetlight casting a warm glow. They looked up at the stars for a moment, gathering their thoughts. This felt like a pivotal moment—a chance to share more than just the surface details.

"You know," Lucas began, glancing at Jamie, "I've never really talked about my upbringing before. It's not something I share easily."

Jamie turned to face them, their expression open and inviting. "You can tell me. I'm here to listen."

Taking a deep breath, Lucas felt a mix of nerves and relief. "I grew up in a rough neighborhood. My family didn't have much, and my parents worked multiple jobs just to keep us afloat. They put everything into giving my siblings and me a better life, but it came with a lot of pressure."

The Weight of Expectations

Lucas's gaze drifted to the sidewalk as memories washed over them. "I was the oldest, and I always felt like I had to be the one to succeed, to be the one who made it out. My parents sacrificed so much for us, and I didn't want to let them down."

They paused, feeling a lump in their throat. "There were times when I trained alone, late at night, when the rest of the world was asleep. I pushed myself harder because I wanted to make them proud, to show them that all their sacrifices were worth it."

Jamie listened intently, nodding slowly. "That's a lot to carry on your shoulders. Did you ever feel like you could just be yourself?"

"Not really," Lucas admitted, their voice barely above a whisper. "It always felt like there was an expectation to uphold. I was so focused on succeeding that I didn't take the time to enjoy the game. It was all about proving myself."

Jamie's expression softened, empathy evident in their eyes. "I understand that pressure. It's tough to navigate the balance between passion and expectations."

Finding Common Ground

As Lucas continued to share, they noticed Jamie's demeanor shifting. "What about you? What's your story?" they asked, genuinely curious.

Jamie hesitated for a moment, then took a deep breath. "I guess I've been under pressure too. My family was supportive, but the expectations from the fans and the media felt suffocating at times. Everyone always has an opinion, and it's hard to tune it out."

"But you've had a lot of success," Lucas said, surprised. "Doesn't that make it easier?"

Jamie shrugged, their smile faltering slightly. "Success doesn't mean you don't struggle. Every time I step on the pitch, I'm afraid of disappointing someone—my family, my teammates, the fans. It's a different kind of pressure."

Building Trust

The honesty in their conversation fostered a sense of trust that both players had been craving. Lucas felt a sense of relief in sharing their truth, realizing they weren't alone in their struggles.

"I wish I had known you earlier," Lucas said, a hint of a smile playing on their lips. "Maybe we could've helped each other out."

"Maybe we still can," Jamie replied, their eyes brightening. "I think we both have a lot to learn from each other."

In that moment, they found a bond rooted in understanding and mutual respect, both acknowledging the difficulties of their paths without judgment. The connection between them deepened, transcending the competitive rivalry that had initially defined their relationship.

A Sense of Hope

As the night grew quieter, Lucas felt a sense of hope swell within them. They realized that sharing their background was not just about unburdening themselves; it was about building a foundation for something more meaningful.

"I appreciate you listening," Lucas said sincerely, feeling lighter than they had in a long time. "It's nice to know that someone else gets it."

"Of course," Jamie replied, their tone warm and reassuring. "We're in this together. And hey, we're not just athletes—we're human too. It's okay to have struggles."

With the air thick with unspoken possibilities, they exchanged a lingering look, the night stretching out before them. Lucas felt a flicker of excitement; perhaps this was the beginning of a deeper connection, one that could shift from rivalry to partnership.

As they walked side by side, a sense of solidarity enveloped them. They were no longer just two players in the Premier League; they were two individuals sharing their vulnerabilities, forging a bond that could withstand the pressures of their world.

A Safe Space

With the atmosphere between them charged with vulnerability, Jamie took a moment to collect their thoughts. The night was serene, a gentle breeze rustling the leaves overhead, and for the first time in a long while, Jamie felt safe to share what lay beneath the surface.

"Since we're being honest," Jamie began, their tone contemplative, "I should tell you about my own struggles. I think you'll get it."

Lucas nodded, leaning in closer, encouraging Jamie to continue. "I'm all ears. What's been weighing on you?"

The Burden of Public Scrutiny

Jamie hesitated, glancing around as if to ensure no one else was listening. "The thing is, everyone sees me as this confident player who has it all figured out. But it's not that simple. I often feel like I'm trapped in this image the public has of me."

Lucas frowned slightly, sensing the seriousness of the moment. "I get that. It's like we have to wear a mask all the time, right?"

"Exactly," Jamie sighed, running a hand through their hair. "I've made mistakes in the past, and they've followed me. Every relationship I've had has been scrutinized, analyzed, and judged. It feels like I can't even breathe without someone commenting on it."

"Must be exhausting," Lucas remarked, their heart aching for the weight Jamie carried. "What happened?"

Revisiting Past Relationships

Jamie took a deep breath, their eyes reflecting a mix of vulnerability and pain. "There was one relationship that really hit me hard. It started out as something beautiful, but the pressures of the public eye and my own insecurities took a toll on it. I was constantly worried about how it would affect my career, and in the end, it crumbled."

"That sounds tough," Lucas replied, their empathy growing. "It's like we're not just playing for ourselves anymore; we're playing for everyone else's expectations too."

"Right," Jamie said, their voice barely above a whisper. "I was so focused on what everyone thought that I lost sight of what I wanted. When it ended, I realized how much I'd let the noise drown out my own feelings. It left me wondering if I could ever truly be happy without the weight of others' opinions."

Lucas felt a knot forming in their stomach, resonating deeply with Jamie's struggles. "It's hard to find a balance when everyone is pulling you in different directions."

Struggling with Self-Identity

Jamie nodded, their eyes clouded with memories. "And it's not just about relationships. I sometimes question my own identity outside of football. When the jersey comes off, who am I? The lines between who I am and who people think I am blur, and I find myself lost in that chaos."

"Wow," Lucas replied, a sense of understanding washing over them. "I can only imagine how confusing that must be. It's hard to navigate those waters when the world is watching you so closely."

"Exactly," Jamie said, their gaze steady. "And the pressure to perform, to be the best version of myself, can be overwhelming. It's like there's always this voice telling me I'm not good enough unless I'm winning trophies or scoring goals."

Finding Common Ground

The honesty in Jamie's words hung in the air, and Lucas felt the intensity of their connection deepen. "I think we're more alike than we realize," Lucas said softly. "I've spent so much time trying to prove myself, not just on the pitch but to everyone who has ever doubted me. It's exhausting, isn't it?"

"It really is," Jamie agreed, a small smile breaking through the heaviness of their conversation. "But talking to you makes me feel less alone. It's nice to finally share this stuff with someone who understands."

"I feel the same way," Lucas replied, their heart swelling with warmth. "It's refreshing to drop the masks we wear and just be ourselves, even if it's just for tonight."

A Bond Strengthened

As they shared their secrets, the connection between them felt like a lifeline in a stormy sea. Jamie realized that the tension they once felt had shifted, replaced by a mutual understanding that transcended the competitive nature of their lives.

"I guess it's a journey for both of us, figuring out who we are beyond football," Jamie said, their voice lighter now.

"Absolutely," Lucas said with a smile. "And who knows? Maybe we can help each other through it."

Jamie chuckled softly, the sound warm and genuine. "I'd like that. It's nice to know I have someone in my corner."

As the night deepened, they continued to share their thoughts, the walls that had once defined their rivalry crumbling away. In the heart of their vulnerabilities, they found the beginnings of a powerful connection, one that could redefine everything they thought they knew about each other.

Chapter 4: The Turning Point

Night Out with Teammates

The night began as a casual outing with teammates to celebrate a recent victory. Laughter and banter filled the air as the group gathered at a lively bar, the atmosphere electric with camaraderie. Lucas and Jamie found themselves side by side, the earlier tensions of rivalry dissipating as they enjoyed each other's company amidst the festivities.

With each round of drinks, the boundaries that once defined them began to blur. The music pulsed around them, a backdrop to the friendly competition of who could tell the funniest story or take the most shots. Lucas noticed how comfortable they felt next to Jamie, the lingering connection from their late-night confessions rekindling warmth between them.

Liquid Courage

As the night progressed, the drinks flowed freely, each one loosening their inhibitions. Jamie laughed at one of Lucas's jokes, their head thrown back in genuine amusement. It was a sound that sent a thrill through Lucas, awakening an unacknowledged desire that had been simmering just below the surface.

"Let's take a shot!" Jamie declared, raising their glass high, eyes sparkling with mischief. Lucas couldn't resist the invitation, joining in with enthusiasm. They clinked glasses, the camaraderie fueling a sense of reckless abandon.

With every shot, the air between them thickened with unspoken tension, the playful glances lingering just a beat longer than necessary. Lucas could feel their heart racing, a mix of excitement and apprehension swirling within.

The Spark Ignites

After a particularly competitive game of darts, their group cheered loudly, and Jamie turned to Lucas, their eyes glinting with challenge. "I bet I can beat you at arm wrestling," they taunted, a playful smirk gracing their lips.

"Is that a challenge?" Lucas replied, their competitive spirit igniting. They moved to a nearby table, laughter and cheers from their teammates surrounding them. As they took their positions, the atmosphere buzzed with anticipation.

In the heat of competition, both players leaned in, their arms straining against each other. Jamie's face was flushed with effort, and Lucas could feel the adrenaline coursing through them. It was in that charged moment, as they locked eyes, that the world around them faded away.

The Moment of No Return

After an intense battle, Lucas finally managed to pin Jamie's arm down, but the victory felt secondary to the electric connection they were sharing. Gasping for breath, they laughed, but the sound shifted to something softer as they maintained eye contact. There was a tension hanging in the air, thick with possibilities, and neither could ignore the pull between them any longer.

Caught in the moment, fueled by the night's revelry, Lucas leaned closer, their heart pounding in their chest. "You're stronger than you look," they said, the words barely escaping their lips.

Jamie smirked, their breath warm against Lucas's skin. "You have no idea what I'm capable of," they replied, their voice low and teasing.

And then it happened. A surge of courage propelled Lucas forward, and their lips met Jamie's in a sudden, unexpected kiss. It was electrifying—wild and passionate, igniting a fire that neither had anticipated.

Caught Off Guard

BREAKING THE RULES

The kiss lasted only a moment, but it felt like an eternity. When they finally pulled apart, both players were breathless, their eyes wide with shock and desire.

"What just happened?" Jamie asked, their tone a mix of confusion and excitement.

"I—uh, I don't know," Lucas stammered, their cheeks flushed. The thrill of the kiss lingered, but so did the uncertainty. "I didn't mean to—"

"No, wait," Jamie interrupted, their expression shifting from surprise to intrigue. "That was... unexpected, but not unwelcome."

Emotional Turmoil

As the reality of the moment sank in, both players stepped back, trying to process the flood of emotions that rushed over them. The kiss had crossed a line, and now they were teetering on the edge of something new and uncertain.

"What does this mean?" Lucas asked, their heart racing with a mix of fear and excitement.

"I don't know," Jamie admitted, running a hand through their hair in frustration. "But I can't pretend that didn't happen. There's something between us, isn't there?"

Lucas nodded, their pulse quickening. "Yeah, there is. But we're rivals. This complicates everything."

"Maybe it does, but it's also kind of thrilling," Jamie replied, their eyes sparkling with mischief. "A little chaos never hurt anyone, right?"

As the night continued, the two players exchanged tentative glances, a newfound tension swirling around them. The kiss had shattered their previous boundaries, leaving them grappling with confusion and desire. They were at a turning point, standing on the precipice of something neither had anticipated.

The Decision Ahead

The laughter of their teammates faded into the background, the world narrowing to just the two of them. Both players knew they had crossed into uncharted territory, and the possibilities that lay ahead filled them with a mix of hope and trepidation.

As they left the bar, the air was charged with uncertainty, but one thing was clear: everything was about to change.

Morning After Realizations

The morning sun streamed through the curtains, illuminating Lucas's room, yet the brightness felt dull compared to the whirlwind of emotions swirling in their mind. As they lay in bed, the events of the previous night flooded back—a night filled with laughter, camaraderie, and that unexpected kiss.

Lucas groaned softly, burying their face in the pillow. "What have I done?" they muttered to themselves. The thrill of the kiss had quickly morphed into a wave of anxiety. The reality of their situation pressed down on them like a weight. They had crossed an unspoken boundary with Jamie, a fellow player and rival, and the implications loomed large.

An Unexpected Encounter

When Lucas arrived at the training facility, their heart raced at the thought of facing Jamie. The atmosphere was charged with the usual competitive energy, but today felt different. Every glance, every interaction felt heavy with unspoken words and unresolved tension.

In the locker room, Jamie was already there, surrounded by teammates. Lucas's pulse quickened at the sight, but they steeled themselves, reminding themselves to keep it casual. "Hey," they greeted, trying to sound nonchalant as they grabbed their gear.

Jamie looked up, their expression a mixture of nervousness and determination. "Hey," they replied, their voice steady but their eyes betraying a hint of uncertainty.

Avoiding the Elephant in the Room

BREAKING THE RULES 31

The rest of the morning passed in a blur, with both players making a conscious effort to act as if nothing had changed. Yet the air crackled with a palpable tension every time their paths crossed. Lucas would catch Jamie's eye only for a moment before looking away, each one hyper-aware of the other's presence.

During practice, they pushed themselves harder than usual, each trying to channel the confusion into their performance. But the more they tried to focus on the game, the more their thoughts drifted back to the kiss—the warmth, the connection, and the undeniable spark that had ignited between them.

Conversations Avoided

As they broke for water, Jamie approached Lucas, who was sitting on the bench, pretending to be engrossed in their phone. "Can we talk?" Jamie asked, a hint of vulnerability in their tone.

"Uh, yeah," Lucas said, suddenly feeling cornered. They glanced around, realizing that their teammates were preoccupied, but the weight of the moment loomed large.

In a quiet corner away from prying eyes, Jamie shifted nervously. "About last night..." they began, their voice hesitant.

Lucas cut in, the fear spilling out. "We don't have to. It was just a kiss, right? Just a moment of... excitement."

"Yeah, but..." Jamie searched for the right words, their brow furrowing in frustration. "It felt like more than just a kiss, and I think we both know it."

"I know," Lucas admitted, their heart racing. "But we can't act on it. Not now. We're rivals, and this could ruin everything."

The Weight of Consequences

Jamie's shoulders slumped, the disappointment palpable. "I get it. But it's hard to just pretend it didn't happen. I felt something, and I don't think I can just ignore that."

"Me neither," Lucas confessed, their voice barely above a whisper. "But think about the team, the fans... it could complicate things in ways we can't even imagine."

Silence hung between them, thick with unspoken fears and desires. Jamie sighed, the fight draining from their shoulders. "So, what do we do? Just go back to how things were before?"

"Maybe that's the best option," Lucas suggested, but the words felt hollow in their chest. "At least for now."

Retreating Emotions

As they returned to the group, the air felt colder, the warmth of their previous connection slipping away like sand through their fingers. Lucas tried to shake off the heaviness of the conversation, but doubt lingered, gnawing at their thoughts.

Later that day, Lucas found themselves lying on their bed again, staring at the ceiling. The kiss replayed in their mind—a perfect moment shattered by the fear of what could come next. They couldn't help but wonder if retreating was the right choice or simply a way to protect themselves from the undeniable truth: they were falling for Jamie, and that was terrifying.

Across town, Jamie was grappling with similar thoughts, pacing their apartment. They replayed the moment of the kiss, the warmth, the electricity, but now it felt like a ghost—an echo of something they longed for but could no longer grasp.

"What if this was it?" they whispered to the empty room. "What if we were meant to be something more, but I let my fears hold me back?"

As they both lay awake in their separate worlds, the weight of their unfulfilled connection pressed down on them. They were at a crossroads, each retreating emotionally, trying to navigate a situation that felt both exhilarating and dangerous.

The truth was undeniable: the kiss had changed everything, and the path ahead was fraught with uncertainty.

Awkward Dynamics

As the days passed, the unspoken tension between Lucas and Jamie began to affect their training. What had once been a lighthearted camaraderie turned into a series of strained interactions, each encounter tinged with an awkwardness that felt both new and uncomfortable.

During practice, Lucas could sense the shift. They noticed how Jamie avoided making eye contact, opting instead to engage with teammates in small talk, leaving Lucas feeling like an outsider in their own circle. It was a familiar isolation, reminiscent of their earlier rivalry, but now it was laced with confusion and unresolved feelings.

The tension reached a boiling point one afternoon during drills. Both players were assigned to the same team, but the usual rhythm they shared felt stilted. Lucas tried to initiate a playful exchange, hoping to break the ice. "Come on, I thought you were supposed to be the best player on the field," they joked, trying to recapture their previous banter.

Jamie shrugged, a distant expression clouding their features. "Yeah, well, I guess I'm just not feeling it today," they replied, their tone flat, leaving Lucas at a loss.

Training Under Pressure

As practice progressed, the competitive edge that once defined their interactions now felt oppressive. Every pass felt heavier, every tackle sharper. Lucas found themselves overthinking every move, conscious of Jamie's presence, and it was affecting their performance.

"Focus, Lucas!" their coach barked during a particularly intense drill, snapping Lucas back to reality. Lucas gritted their teeth, feeling the pressure mount. They caught Jamie's eye for just a moment, but instead of the spark they had once shared, there was only silence—a chasm growing between them.

After practice, Jamie approached Lucas in the locker room, the tension palpable. "You're not playing like yourself," Jamie observed, their brow furrowed with concern.

"I'm fine," Lucas replied, perhaps a little too quickly. "Just trying to get into the right headspace for the upcoming match."

Jamie crossed their arms, a mixture of frustration and sympathy in their expression. "You can't keep pretending everything's okay. It's not. This awkwardness is killing our game."

Confronting the Issue

The conversation hung in the air like a thick fog, neither wanting to dive deeper into the emotional quagmire that lay beneath. But Jamie couldn't ignore the truth any longer. "Look, I know we're both avoiding the elephant in the room," they said, taking a step closer. "But I don't want to keep pretending that nothing happened. We need to talk about it."

Lucas felt their heart race, the urge to deflect rising within them. "What's there to talk about? We kissed. It was a mistake, right? We're rivals—this complicates everything."

Jamie shook their head, their expression earnest. "No, it wasn't just a mistake. It meant something. At least to me."

Emotions Unleashed

The admission hung heavily between them, igniting a mixture of hope and fear in Lucas. "It did?" they asked, the vulnerability in their voice unmistakable.

"Yeah," Jamie admitted, their voice softening. "I felt something real, and it's been driving me crazy trying to figure it all out while pretending we can just go back to being rivals."

Lucas's defenses crumbled slightly at the honesty. "I felt it too," they confessed, their heart pounding. "But I'm scared. Scared of what it means for us, for our careers, for everything we've worked for."

"I'm scared too," Jamie replied, their eyes locking onto Lucas's. "But maybe we can figure it out together. I don't want to lose what we have just because we kissed."

A Pivotal Moment

As they stood there, the weight of their words settling between them, Lucas felt a flicker of hope ignite in their chest. "So what do we do?" they asked, their voice trembling with uncertainty.

Jamie took a deep breath, their expression resolute. "Let's not rush into anything. We can take our time to figure out what this is. But we need to be honest with each other, both on and off the field."

The promise hung in the air, a fragile agreement that felt like a lifeline. Both players understood the challenge ahead: navigating their feelings while maintaining the competitive spirit that drove them.

Strengthening Bonds

As they left the locker room, there was a renewed sense of determination between them. The awkwardness remained, but now it felt different—less like an insurmountable wall and more like a hurdle they could overcome together.

During the next training session, Lucas noticed a shift in their dynamic. There was still tension, but it was underpinned by a sense of mutual understanding. They shared glances that lingered a second too long, and playful banter began to creep back into their interactions, slowly eroding the unease that had defined the days before.

With every passing moment, Lucas and Jamie began to rediscover the bond that had initially drawn them together. They were still rivals on the field, but the lines were beginning to blur, giving way to a deeper connection that neither of them had expected.

As they both took a moment to reflect on their journey, Lucas realized that the tension wasn't just a burden; it was also a testament to their growing feelings, and maybe—just maybe—it was the beginning of something extraordinary.

Chapter 5: The Media Storm

Caught Off Guard

The sun dipped low in the sky as Lucas and Jamie left the training facility together, the air crackling with the unspoken promise of their evolving friendship. They had spent the afternoon discussing strategies for the upcoming match, but the conversation had drifted into more personal territory, filled with laughter and shared dreams.

As they walked to their cars, engrossed in conversation, neither player noticed the flash of cameras hidden in the shadows. Paparazzi, ever vigilant, were lurking nearby, always on the lookout for a scoop.

When the first flash went off, Lucas turned abruptly, squinting into the light. "What the—" They instinctively stepped closer to Jamie, a reflexive move to shield their friend, but the closeness only drew more attention from the lurking photographers.

"Just keep walking," Jamie murmured, an edge of anxiety in their voice. They moved toward their respective vehicles, but the damage was already done.

Headlines Explode

Within hours, social media was abuzz. Pictures of the two players standing close together, smiles on their faces, were plastered across various tabloids and online platforms. Headlines screamed speculation: "Is This the Premier League's Hottest New Couple?" and "Rivalry or Romance? Inside the Relationship of Lucas and Jamie!"

Lucas's phone buzzed incessantly with notifications, each ping a reminder of the whirlwind that had just begun. They felt a mix of embarrassment and anger as they scrolled through the articles, each one digging deeper into their personal lives, speculating about their relationship and what the paparazzi had captured.

"Did you see this?" Lucas exclaimed, turning to Jamie as they both settled into their cars. "This is ridiculous! We're not even dating!"

"I know," Jamie replied, rubbing the back of their neck in frustration. "But you know how the media is. They thrive on this kind of drama."

Confronting the Rumors

The next day, the impact of the media storm hit them both hard during training. Teammates threw knowing glances their way, and whispers followed them like shadows.

"Looks like you two are getting cozy," one teammate joked, nudging Lucas with a playful grin. Lucas forced a laugh, but inside, they felt a knot of anxiety tighten.

Jamie stepped forward, their voice steady. "It's just a rumor. We were talking, that's all."

"Sure," the teammate replied, but the teasing tone lingered, leaving Lucas feeling exposed and vulnerable. They exchanged a glance with Jamie, the understanding that they were now both in the spotlight making their bond feel even more complicated.

After practice, they found a moment alone in the locker room. Lucas paced, frustration bubbling beneath the surface. "I can't believe this is happening. We can't even talk without the world speculating about us."

Jamie leaned against the wall, their expression thoughtful. "Maybe we should just own it? If they think we're dating, let's not hide it. It might take some of the pressure off."

Lucas paused, contemplating the suggestion. "Are you serious? You want to fuel the rumors?"

"Not fuel them," Jamie clarified, pushing off the wall to face Lucas fully. "But if we're going to be seen together, we might as well make it clear that we're okay with it. Maybe it'll give us a little freedom to figure things out without the constant scrutiny."

Navigating the Fallout

The next few days brought a frenzy of attention. Every public appearance, every social media post, felt like an open invitation for speculation. The paparazzi followed them relentlessly, and soon, both players were forced to navigate a new reality where their every move was documented and dissected.

At a post-match press conference, Lucas could feel the weight of the cameras as they answered questions about the game. The journalists, eager for a soundbite, zeroed in on the recent headlines.

"Can you clarify your relationship with Jamie?" one reporter pressed, leaning forward eagerly.

Lucas exchanged a quick glance with Jamie, who sat beside them, their jaw set in determination. "We're friends," Lucas said, striving for calm. "We've known each other for years, and we're just trying to support one another."

But as the questions continued, Jamie added, "Look, we're both adults, and we can have personal relationships outside of the field. Whatever people want to speculate about is their business, but our focus is on the game."

Defining Their Narrative

After the press conference, Lucas and Jamie found themselves in the same quiet corner of the training facility where they often had their serious talks.

"Do you think that was enough?" Lucas asked, a mixture of concern and hope in their eyes.

Jamie shrugged, a faint smile appearing. "Maybe. But we can't control what people think. What matters is how we handle it together."

"Together," Lucas repeated, feeling the warmth of that word settle in their chest. "I like the sound of that."

As they walked out of the training center, Lucas felt a renewed sense of resolve. They were navigating uncharted territory, but with Jamie by their side, they were ready to face whatever the media storm would throw their way.

Together, they would redefine their narrative—one based on their choices, not the whispers of tabloids. And as they embraced the challenge, Lucas couldn't shake the feeling that this moment, though chaotic, was another step toward solidifying their bond, whatever shape it might take.

Scrutiny and Speculation

As the days unfolded after the initial wave of rumors, the backlash intensified. Fans of both players reacted in wildly different ways, some expressing support for their supposed romance, while others were outraged by the mere suggestion of a relationship between rivals. Social media became a battleground, with hashtags trending, and debates erupting across platforms.

Lucas scrolled through their timeline, heart sinking at the harsh comments. "#NotMyPlayer" was trending, filled with vitriol from fans who believed their favorite athlete should maintain a certain image. "How could he betray us?" one comment read, while another questioned Lucas's commitment to the team.

Feeling overwhelmed, Lucas tossed their phone onto the couch, frustration boiling over. "This is insane! I didn't ask for any of this. I'm just trying to do my job!"

Jamie, who had been pacing the room, paused and turned to face Lucas, concern etched on their features. "I know it's a lot. But we can't let it get to us. We have to focus on what we can control."

Intense Pressure

During the next match, the atmosphere was electric but tense. The stadium buzzed with fans, some wearing shirts emblazoned with the players' names side by side, while others held up signs proclaiming their disdain for the rumors.

Every time Lucas touched the ball, a wave of cheers and boos erupted, making it impossible to concentrate. The pressure mounted, and Lucas felt their heart race, each play a reflection of the turmoil swirling in their mind.

Jamie sensed the strain and tried to offer support during a break in the action. "Hey, just remember why we're here. It's about the game, not the drama."

Lucas nodded, but the weight of the public scrutiny hung heavily on them. "It's hard to separate it all, B. Everyone is watching us, waiting for us to fail."

Conflicting Emotions

As the game progressed, Lucas struggled to find their rhythm. Mistakes were made, and the anxiety bubbled to the surface. A missed pass here, a fumbled tackle there—it all compounded the stress. With each misstep, the whispers in the stadium grew louder, and Lucas could feel the judgment of fans pressing down on them like a heavy cloak.

At halftime, the players retreated to the locker room, and the tension was palpable. Lucas sat in silence, feeling a mixture of embarrassment and anger well up inside them.

"Hey," Jamie said, crouching down beside Lucas, their voice low and calming. "Don't let them get to you. You know you're better than this."

Lucas looked up, eyes filled with uncertainty. "But what if I'm not? What if all this noise is messing with my game? I don't want to let my team down."

"You're not letting anyone down," Jamie replied firmly. "You're here for a reason. Just remember that."

The sincerity in Jamie's eyes broke through the haze of doubt, but the conflicting emotions still churned within Lucas. They felt torn between their growing feelings for Jamie and the overwhelming pressure of public perception.

A Turning Point on the Field

The second half began, and Lucas stepped onto the pitch, determination flooding their veins. The noise of the crowd faded, and all they could focus on was the game. They played with a fierce intensity, pouring all their energy into every pass and every tackle.

Jamie was right there alongside them, matching their efforts and pushing them forward. With every successful play, Lucas could feel a flicker of confidence returning, the bond between them growing stronger in the heat of competition.

As the clock ticked down, Lucas found themselves in a crucial moment—a breakaway opportunity. The goal was within reach, and they felt the weight of the moment settle on their shoulders. They took a deep breath, recalled Jamie's encouraging words, and charged forward.

The ball soared into the net, a clean shot that echoed through the stadium. Cheers erupted, drowning out the previous tension. In that instant, Lucas felt a surge of triumph, not just for scoring but for reclaiming their spirit.

Aftermath of the Match

After the final whistle blew, they celebrated with their teammates, but Lucas's gaze quickly found Jamie across the field. The jubilant atmosphere faded as they locked eyes, both players understanding the silent exchange—their shared struggles and victories mirrored in that moment.

But as they left the field, the weight of public perception came crashing back. They were met with a throng of reporters eager for their take on the match—and the speculation surrounding their relationship.

"Can you comment on your chemistry on and off the field?" a reporter shouted, thrusting a microphone in Lucas's direction.

Lucas exchanged a glance with Jamie, both recognizing the familiar tension returning. "We're focused on the game," Lucas replied, their voice steady. "That's all that matters right now."

As they walked away, Jamie leaned closer. "That was good. You handled it well."

"Thanks," Lucas said, though doubts lingered in their mind. The scrutiny was only going to intensify, and navigating the storm ahead would require more than just skill on the field.

Facing the Backlash Together

In the days following the match, the media frenzy showed no signs of slowing down. New headlines emerged, dissecting their every move, questioning their professionalism, and demanding answers about their relationship.

Lucas and Jamie faced intense pressure from fans and pundits alike, each new article amplifying their anxiety. They spent hours discussing strategies to cope with the backlash, working together to find a balance between their personal lives and professional aspirations.

One evening, as they sat in Lucas's living room, the tension hung thick in the air. Jamie finally broke the silence. "We need to address this head-on. We can't let them dictate our narrative."

Lucas nodded, heart racing at the thought of a public statement. "You're right. But how do we do that without making it worse?"

"Together," Jamie replied, determination in their eyes. "We'll frame it in our own words. We owe it to ourselves and to our fans."

And as they plotted their course forward, Lucas felt a surge of hope amidst the chaos. They were no longer just navigating the storm individually—they were a team, ready to face whatever came next, hand in hand.

The Weight of Words

The media storm reached a fever pitch, and both players felt the pressure building. A few days after the match, they found themselves alone in the training facility, the atmosphere thick with tension. Lucas paced back and forth, their brow furrowed in frustration.

"I can't believe you said that in the interview," Lucas shot, stopping to face Jamie. "You didn't have to acknowledge the rumors at all!"

Jamie crossed their arms, leaning against the wall with a sigh. "And what, pretend they don't exist? That's not realistic. We can't just ignore it; it's affecting our careers and our reputations."

"But you made it sound like it's something real," Lucas argued, voice rising. "You're the one who put it out there. You don't get it, do you? This isn't just about us. It's about everything we've worked for!"

Challenging Perspectives

Jamie pushed off the wall, moving closer. "No, you don't get it! This is exactly why I didn't want to hide anything. Love isn't something to be ashamed of. Why should we let public perception dictate how we feel?"

Lucas felt their pulse quicken, the adrenaline of their argument blending with the confusion of their emotions. "It's not about shame, Jamie! It's about the risk. You think I want to deal with the backlash from fans who don't understand? They'll tear us apart, and it'll ruin everything we've built!"

"So what? You're willing to sacrifice your happiness just to please the fans? You'd rather play by their rules than be true to yourself?" Jamie challenged, their voice steady but passionate.

Lucas's heart raced as they grappled with the reality of their feelings. "This isn't just about happiness. It's about our careers, our livelihoods! We're public figures; we can't just fall in love and expect everything to be fine. The stakes are too high!"

Emotional Explosion

The air crackled with tension, both players on the brink of an emotional explosion. Jamie stepped back, frustration evident in their posture. "You act like I'm the one risking everything here. But maybe you're the one who doesn't want to face what we have. Is that it?"

Lucas recoiled slightly, caught off guard by the accusation. "How can you even say that? You think I'm running away? I just want to protect what we have—what we've built together!"

Jamie shook their head, disbelief etched on their face. "By denying it? By pretending it's not there? That's not protecting anything; it's suffocating it. You can't love someone and also keep them hidden in the shadows."

Silence hung heavy in the air, both players breathing heavily as the weight of their argument settled around them. Lucas felt their defenses crumble under Jamie's fierce gaze, the hurt in their eyes cutting deeper than any words.

A Moment of Reflection

Lucas turned away, taking a deep breath to gather their thoughts. "I'm scared, okay? I've never felt this way about anyone before. The stakes feel so high. If this doesn't work out, it could destroy everything for both of us."

Jamie's expression softened, sensing the vulnerability beneath Lucas's bravado. "And what if it does work out? What if this is the best thing that's ever happened to us? You can't let fear dictate your life, A. Love is worth the risk."

After a moment of silence, Lucas finally faced Jamie, their eyes searching for understanding. "But is it worth the chaos that comes with it? The media storm, the judgment, the fans? What if it changes everything we've known?"

Finding Common Ground

Jamie stepped closer, their voice dropping to a softer tone. "You know what's really chaotic? Hiding who we are. Living in fear of what others think. If we can weather the storm together, we'll be stronger for it. We owe it to ourselves to at least try."

Lucas felt the tension begin to ease, their heart racing with a mixture of fear and hope. "You really believe that?"

"I do," Jamie replied earnestly. "But we need to face it together. We can't let them tear us apart before we even give this a chance."

With the confrontation hanging in the air, Lucas nodded slowly, recognizing the truth in Jamie's words. "Okay, let's try. But we have to be careful. This isn't going to be easy."

Jamie smiled, a glimmer of hope lighting up their expression. "We'll take it one day at a time. Together."

A New Beginning

As they stood there, the weight of the argument shifting into a shared understanding, Lucas felt a flicker of excitement spark within them. The journey ahead wouldn't be easy, but with Jamie by their side, they were ready to face whatever challenges lay ahead.

In that moment, amidst the backdrop of a brewing media storm, both players knew they had crossed a line—into a territory where love and fame intertwined, forcing them to confront not just the external pressures but their own fears and desires.

With their hearts open, they took the first step toward embracing their new reality, ready to weather the storm together.

Chapter 6: Heartbreak and Misunderstandings

The Photo Leak

It started as a typical match day, filled with adrenaline and the roar of the crowd. But when Lucas arrived home after a hard-fought game, they found their phone flooded with notifications. Scrolling through the messages, one caught their eye—a photo that made their stomach drop.

It was a picture of Jamie, standing closely with a female reporter during a post-match interview, their body language relaxed and intimate. The caption, accompanied by a sensational headline, insinuated that Jamie was moving on from their recent relationship with Lucas.

"Are you serious?" Lucas muttered, their heart sinking as they read the comments pouring in from fans and media alike. The internet buzzed with speculation, and a wave of jealousy washed over them, quickly mingling with a sense of betrayal.

Confrontation in the Locker Room

The following day, the team gathered in the locker room, the air thick with anticipation. Lucas's frustration simmered beneath the surface as they spotted Jamie laughing with teammates, seemingly unfazed by the chaos unfolding outside.

Unable to contain their feelings, Lucas approached Jamie, their heart racing with anger and hurt. "We need to talk."

Jamie turned, surprised by the tone in Lucas's voice. "What's wrong?"

"Did you even see the photo? You look cozy with that reporter!" Lucas snapped, crossing their arms defensively.

Jamie's expression shifted from confusion to concern. "A, it was nothing! I was just answering questions after the match. You know how the media can twist things."

"I don't know what to believe anymore," Lucas retorted, their voice rising. "It seems like you're more interested in playing the game than in us."

Jamie's brows furrowed, hurt creeping into their voice. "How can you say that? I thought we were on the same page. I thought you trusted me."

Emotional Fallout

Lucas shook their head, the weight of insecurity crashing down on them. "It's hard to trust when all I see is you with someone else. How can I not feel like I'm just another headline to you?"

"This isn't about you being a headline!" Jamie argued, their frustration evident. "It's about a moment taken out of context! Why can't you see that? You're letting the media dictate how you feel!"

The argument escalated, voices rising until the entire locker room was silent, all eyes on the two players. The tension was palpable, with teammates exchanging concerned glances.

"Maybe you're right," Lucas spat, their voice cracking with emotion. "Maybe I can't handle this after all."

"Don't say that," Jamie pleaded, stepping closer. "You're the one I care about. I didn't ask for any of this!"

"But you're the one in the spotlight," Lucas shot back, hurt spilling over. "I'm just trying to figure out where I fit in all of this."

The Aftermath

With that, Lucas stormed out of the locker room, the weight of the misunderstanding bearing down on their shoulders. The air outside felt heavy, as if the world around them was closing in.

Jamie stood frozen, feeling a mix of anger and despair. They hadn't meant for it to escalate this way, but now they were left grappling with the fallout of a relationship that seemed to teeter on the edge.

As days passed, Lucas avoided Jamie at training, their heart filled with confusion and hurt. The media frenzy continued to swirl, amplifying the misunderstandings that festered between them.

A Call for Clarity

Desperate to make sense of the chaos, Lucas reached out to a close friend, pouring out their feelings over coffee. "I don't know what to do. One moment, everything feels right, and the next, I'm second-guessing everything."

Jamie, on the other hand, sought advice from a trusted teammate, who urged them to reach out and communicate. "You can't let this fester. If you really care, you need to clear the air."

Both players felt the weight of their unspoken words, the misunderstandings threatening to pull them apart. But the question lingered: Could they find a way to bridge the gap, or was this the beginning of the end?

A Decision to Face the Truth

Finally, Lucas found the courage to send a message to Jamie, requesting a private meeting. They knew they needed to confront their emotions and fears head-on if they wanted to salvage what they had begun to build.

When they met, the tension was palpable. Lucas took a deep breath, their heart racing. "We need to talk. I don't want to lose you over something that was never real to begin with."

Jamie nodded, their expression softening. "I feel the same way. I didn't mean to hurt you. Can we just be honest about everything?"

As they stood together, both players understood that the misunderstandings and heartbreak were part of a larger journey—one that would either forge their bond or tear them apart.

Isolation in the Spotlight

In the aftermath of the confrontation, Lucas retreated into a shell of their own making. The vibrant colors of their life faded to a dull gray as they focused solely on training. Each morning began with the same routine: wake up, hit the gym, train with the team, and then head home to solitude. The exhilaration of the game had been replaced by a gnawing emptiness.

While the rest of the team engaged in laughter and camaraderie, Lucas felt like an outsider looking in. They kept their head down, pushing through drills with mechanical precision, determined to drown out the noise of their heartache. Every time Jamie approached, attempting to reach out, Lucas's stomach twisted with a mix of anger and hurt, and they would turn away.

The Toll of Silence

Days turned into weeks, and the tension became a suffocating silence that filled the air. Teammates began to notice the shift; whispers spread among them about the rift between the two stars. The media, ever hungry for drama, seized on the opportunity, crafting headlines that only deepened the divide.

Lucas, scrolling through social media after practice, couldn't escape the barrage of opinions. Fans speculated wildly about their relationship, some defending Lucas while others accused them of being jealous and insecure. Each comment felt like a dagger, further isolating them from the team and their own emotions.

During team meetings, Lucas sat apart, eyes trained on the floor, unable to meet anyone's gaze. Training sessions became grueling exercises in avoidance, and Lucas found solace only in the rhythmic pounding of their feet on the pitch. Football was their escape, a temporary reprieve from the turmoil inside.

Confronting Inner Demons

At night, however, when the stadium lights dimmed and silence enveloped the world, the loneliness crept back in. Lucas would lie awake, staring at the ceiling, wrestling with their thoughts. Memories of laughter shared with Jamie, the warmth of their bond, and the passion of their late-night confessions haunted them.

"Why am I pushing them away?" Lucas whispered into the darkness, frustration and sorrow mixing into a painful knot in their chest. "Why can't I just talk to them?"

But the thought of facing Jamie filled them with dread. What if they were right? What if Jamie really did care less than they claimed? The fear of being vulnerable was paralyzing.

A Moment of Weakness

One evening, overwhelmed by emotions, Lucas found themselves sitting alone on a park bench near the stadium. The sun dipped below the horizon, painting the sky with shades of orange and pink, yet it felt like the light had vanished from their world.

As they scrolled through their phone, an alert popped up—a video interview featuring Jamie discussing the fallout from the misunderstanding. Lucas's heart raced as they clicked on it, unable to look away.

In the video, Jamie spoke candidly about their feelings, the hurt from the recent events evident in their eyes. "I never wanted to hurt A. We had something real, and it feels like it's slipping away because of all this noise. I just want them to understand that I'm here, that I care."

Lucas's heart ached at the raw honesty in Jamie's voice. They could see the pain reflected in Jamie's expression, and for the first time, doubt flickered in their mind. Had they misread the situation? Had their jealousy blinded them to Jamie's genuine feelings?

The Decision to Open Up

Feeling the weight of their emotions crashing down, Lucas left the park and headed home. The conflict inside them reached a boiling point. They couldn't continue like this, trapped in a cycle of anger and misunderstanding.

As they lay in bed that night, a determination began to settle within. "I can't keep running," they whispered to the darkness. "I have to face this head-on. I owe it to us."

The next morning, Lucas woke with a new resolve. They had to reach out to Jamie, to break the silence that had grown between them. It wouldn't be easy, but they were ready to confront their fears and the truth of their feelings.

Reaching Out

Taking a deep breath, Lucas picked up their phone and typed out a message. "Can we talk? I think we need to clear the air. I'm sorry for pushing you away."

After hitting send, Lucas felt a mix of anxiety and hope. Would Jamie even want to talk after everything that had happened? Would they be willing to let go of the hurt?

Moments later, a reply came through. "I'd like that. When and where?"

Relief flooded over Lucas, and they quickly arranged to meet at their favorite café. As the time approached, their heart raced with anticipation and fear. They knew they were about to open a door to a conversation that could either heal them or push them further apart.

The Weight of Absence

As the days passed, Jamie felt the sharp edge of absence biting deeper. The silence between them was deafening, each missed connection amplifying the distance that had grown like a chasm. Training sessions felt unfulfilling without the banter and camaraderie they had once shared with Lucas. Instead of the usual excitement, every drill was tinged with a sense of loss.

During warm-ups, Jamie caught themselves glancing over, half-expecting to see Lucas's familiar figure, their laughter echoing in the air. But every time they looked, the spot remained empty, and an ache settled in their chest. "What have I done?" they whispered to themselves, replaying their last argument over and over, the harsh words echoing in their mind.

Conversations with Teammates

During a break in training, Jamie found solace in their teammates' company, but even their light-hearted jokes fell flat. They exchanged worried glances, sensing that something was off. A close friend approached, concern etched on their face. "You've been quiet lately, B. Is everything okay with A?"

Jamie sighed, running a hand through their hair. "I don't know. I just feel... lost. It's like everything we had has vanished."

Their friend nodded, understanding the weight of the situation. "Have you tried talking to them? Sometimes you have to be the first to reach out, even when it's hard."

"I know," Jamie replied, guilt pooling in their stomach. "I just don't want to make things worse. I thought giving them space would help, but it's only made me realize how much I care."

Late Nights and Inner Turmoil

At night, when the world quieted, Jamie found it impossible to escape their thoughts. Lying awake in bed, they replayed the moments they had shared with Lucas: the laughter, the shared dreams of success, the deep conversations that felt like they could last forever. Each memory felt like a bittersweet reminder of what they had lost.

Jamie sat up, the moonlight streaming through their window, casting shadows across the room. "Why did I let my pride get in the way?" they muttered, frustration boiling within them. "I should have fought harder for us."

The realization hit like a wave, washing over them with clarity. The distance they had created was unbearable, and the more they reflected, the more they understood the depth of their feelings. "I love A," Jamie whispered into the darkness, the admission both freeing and terrifying.

A Call to Action

With this newfound clarity came a surge of determination. They couldn't remain idle, trapped in regret while Lucas likely felt the same pain. Jamie picked up their phone, staring at the screen where Lucas's contact name glowed in the dark.

"Just do it," they urged themselves, fingers hovering over the keyboard. "You can't let fear win."

They typed a message, their heart racing with each word. "A, can we meet? I need to talk about everything. I miss you."

After hitting send, Jamie felt a mix of anxiety and hope. Would Lucas respond? Would they be willing to hear Jamie out after everything that had happened?

The Response

Minutes felt like hours as Jamie waited for a reply, the tension building within them. When the notification finally pinged, they nearly dropped the phone in anticipation.

"Of course. Let's meet at the café tomorrow."

Relief flooded over Jamie, but along with it came a new wave of anxiety. They had to be honest this time, to lay their feelings bare without fear. They knew this was their chance to confront their mistakes and fight for the love that had blossomed against all odds.

Preparing for the Meeting

The next day, as Jamie prepared to meet Lucas, they took a moment to reflect in the mirror. "You can do this," they reassured themselves, practicing their words silently. "Just speak from the heart. Be vulnerable."

They arrived at the café early, nerves coursing through them like electricity. The familiar aroma of coffee filled the air, but it did little to calm their racing heart. As they waited, Jamie felt the weight of their choices pressing down, but the thought of finally addressing their feelings gave them hope.

When Lucas walked in, their expression cautious yet hopeful, Jamie's heart leapt. This was their moment. The distance had been painful, but it had also led them to a profound understanding of their love. Now, they just had to find the right words to express it.

Chapter 7: The Comeback

A Heartfelt Plan

As the date of the crucial match approached, Jamie's determination solidified into a plan. They knew they needed to make a grand gesture, something that would not only show Lucas their unwavering support but also symbolize their love. After a sleepless night of brainstorming, an idea formed—a plan that combined passion, vulnerability, and a touch of bravery.

Standing in front of the mirror, Jamie practiced their speech. "I believe in you, A. I want everyone to know how much you mean to me," they said aloud, feeling the weight of their commitment with each word. The idea of wearing a personalized jersey, emblazoned with Lucas's name and their own number as a show of solidarity, filled them with both excitement and trepidation.

The Day of the Match

Match day arrived, electric with anticipation. The stadium buzzed with energy, fans clad in team colors, chanting and cheering for their heroes. Jamie felt a mix of nerves and exhilaration as they prepared for the game. They could sense the pressure surrounding the players, especially Lucas, who had been under a spotlight due to the rumors and the fallout from their misunderstanding.

Arriving at the stadium, Jamie donned the specially designed jersey—a bold statement piece that showcased Lucas's name across the back, with their own number prominently displayed on the front. They added a simple but meaningful touch: a heart symbol stitched near the hem, a secret between them that spoke volumes.

As they walked through the bustling crowds, cheers erupted, but Jamie's focus remained on the field where Lucas was warming up. The tension was palpable, but they felt a rush of determination. They were ready to bridge the gap that had grown between them.

In the Stands

The game kicked off, and Jamie found their seat among the throng of fans. As the match progressed, they cheered enthusiastically, trying to catch Lucas's eye. Every play, every goal attempt felt intensified by the weight of their feelings. Lucas played with a fire that had been missing in previous games, fueled perhaps by the knowledge that Jamie was there, supporting them.

As the minutes ticked down, the tension reached a breaking point. The opposing team scored, sending shockwaves through the stadium. Lucas's frustration was palpable, their competitive nature ignited. But Jamie remained resolute, shouting encouragement, waving their arms to catch Lucas's attention. "You got this, Lucas! Show them what you're made of!"

The Turning Point

As the clock wound down, Lucas looked up, their gaze scanning the crowd until it landed on Jamie. A flicker of surprise crossed Lucas's face, quickly replaced by a smile that ignited warmth in Jamie's chest. In that moment, everything felt possible again.

With renewed energy, Lucas dove back into the game, displaying incredible skill and determination. They maneuvered past defenders, their focus laser-sharp, driven by the support from the stands. The team rallied behind Lucas's infectious energy, and together, they pushed toward a comeback.

With only minutes left, the tension reached its peak. Lucas received the ball in a crucial moment, and the stadium held its breath. Jamie stood, heart racing, chanting Lucas's name along with the crowd. "Lucas! Lucas! Lucas!"

The Winning Goal

BREAKING THE RULES   57

In a breathtaking moment, Lucas found an opening and launched a powerful shot toward the goal. Time seemed to freeze as the ball soared through the air, a beautiful arc that ended with a triumphant net ripple. The stadium erupted in a deafening roar, fans leaping to their feet, celebrating the incredible comeback.

Jamie was swept up in the euphoria, but their focus remained on Lucas, who turned to the stands, eyes bright with victory. When Lucas spotted Jamie in the crowd, wearing the jersey, their expression shifted from elation to something deeper—recognition, gratitude, and love.

THE AFTERMATH

As the celebrations continued, Jamie waited for Lucas to approach, adrenaline coursing through their veins. They knew this moment was pivotal—a chance to reconnect and rebuild what had been strained.

When Lucas finally made their way through the throngs of cheering fans, the joy in their eyes was unmistakable. "You came!" Lucas exclaimed, breathless from the game and the exhilaration of the crowd.

"I wanted you to know I'm here for you, no matter what," Jamie replied, a mix of nerves and excitement swirling within them. "I believe in you, A. And I believe in us."

The tension that had once felt insurmountable now hung in the air, charged with unspoken emotions. The weight of their misunderstandings began to lift, replaced by the promise of reconciliation. As the crowds began to disperse, Jamie felt the path to healing opening before them, filled with possibilities and hope.

Post-Match Euphoria

As the final whistle blew and the crowd erupted into cheers, Jamie felt a wave of exhilaration wash over them. The energy in the stadium was infectious, but their heart raced for a different reason. The victory was monumental, but it was the moment spent sharing that win with

Lucas that felt even more significant. They watched as the players celebrated on the field, but all Jamie could focus on was finding Lucas amidst the throngs of teammates and fans.

As the excitement began to dissipate, Jamie navigated through the sea of jubilant supporters, their heart pounding with a mixture of hope and anxiety. They needed to talk to Lucas, to express everything they had bottled up since their misunderstanding. It was time to lay it all on the table.

A Private Moment

Eventually, Jamie spotted Lucas standing off to the side, still in their gear, surrounded by a few fans and reporters. As they approached, Lucas's laughter echoed in the air, but there was an undercurrent of something deeper—an intensity that drew Jamie closer.

When the crowd began to thin, Jamie seized the opportunity, stepping forward. "A, can we talk?" Their voice was steady, but inside, nerves danced with anticipation.

Lucas turned, surprise flashing across their face, quickly replaced by a soft smile. "Of course. I was hoping you would come find me."

They moved to a quieter corner of the stadium, away from the remaining fans. The atmosphere felt charged, a mix of victory and the unspoken tension that had been building between them. Lucas leaned against a nearby wall, their expression shifting from jubilance to something more contemplative as they met Jamie's gaze.

Finding the Right Words

Taking a deep breath, Jamie gathered their thoughts. "I know things have been complicated between us," they began, their voice earnest. "After everything that happened, I realized how much I care about you—more than I ever let on."

Lucas's eyes softened, the flicker of understanding shining through. "I feel the same way, but it's been hard to navigate all of this. The pressure from the media, the fans... it's overwhelming."

Nodding, Jamie continued, "I thought giving you space was the right thing to do, but the more time passed, the more I missed you. I don't want to lose what we have because of misunderstandings or fears. You mean too much to me."

Vulnerability Unveiled

Lucas took a step closer, vulnerability etched in their features. "I didn't want to admit how much I care about you either. I was scared. Scared of what it would mean for us, especially with everything happening around us." Their voice trembled slightly, revealing the depth of their emotions.

Jamie's heart ached at the sight of Lucas's struggle. "I know the stakes are high, but I believe we can face anything together. You make me feel alive, A. It's not just about football; it's about us, and I want to fight for that."

The honesty of Jamie's words hung in the air, weaving through the tension like a lifeline. Lucas looked down for a moment, processing the confession, and Jamie could see the internal battle waging in their mind.

The Moment of Truth

Finally, Lucas raised their gaze, their eyes shimmering with unshed emotion. "I've felt lost without you, and the truth is, I love you, B. I didn't know how to say it without putting everything at risk."

The admission sparked a warmth within Jamie, and a smile broke through their earlier tension. "I love you too, A. I always have. I want to be there for you, in every way—on and off the field."

Lucas's face lit up with a mixture of relief and joy. They took another step forward, closing the distance between them. "Then let's stop hiding from what we feel. Let's face whatever comes together, no matter how tough it gets."

Sealing Their Commitment

With the weight of unspoken emotions lifted, Jamie reached out, cupping Lucas's face in their hands. "Together," they affirmed, their voices almost a whisper, a promise shared between them.

In that intimate moment, they leaned in, their lips brushing softly against one another, hesitant at first but growing in confidence. The kiss was electric, igniting a spark that had been dormant for too long. It was more than just a seal of their feelings; it was a reaffirmation of their connection amidst the chaos that surrounded them.

As they pulled away, breathless and smiling, Lucas's eyes sparkled with renewed hope. "We'll navigate this together, B. I know we can."

"Together," Jamie echoed, feeling a sense of peace wash over them. In that moment, surrounded by the echoes of victory and the lingering buzz of the crowd, they knew they had turned a corner. The journey ahead wouldn't be easy, but they were ready to face it side by side.

An Understanding

The lingering warmth from their kiss enveloped Jamie as they took a step back, feeling the weight of the moment settle around them. The chaos of the match faded into the background, leaving just the two of them standing amidst the echoes of the crowd, a newfound clarity radiating between them.

"I can't believe how scared I was to talk to you," Lucas admitted, their voice barely above a whisper, as if afraid to break the fragile spell of their reunion. "I let the fear of what others would think hold me back."

Jamie smiled, understanding the vulnerability that came with their shared world of fame and expectations. "I felt the same way. I thought if I just stayed quiet, I could protect us. But hiding only made things worse. I want to face the challenges with you, A."

Lucas nodded, a spark of determination lighting their eyes. "You're right. We've spent so long building walls around our feelings, fearing what could happen if we let anyone in. But now, I see that we can't let fear dictate our relationship. Our love is worth fighting for, no matter the consequences."

Setting Boundaries

Jamie took a deep breath, feeling a rush of hope. "So, what do we do now? How do we navigate all this? The media, the fans... they're relentless."

With a newfound confidence, Lucas replied, "We set boundaries. We control the narrative. We go public about us on our terms, not anyone else's. We don't owe them anything, but we owe it to ourselves to be honest about who we are."

Jamie felt their heart swell at Lucas's words. The thought of being able to embrace their love openly was both exhilarating and terrifying. "That sounds perfect, but are you ready for the fallout? There will be questions, assumptions... and I'm not sure how people will react."

Lucas smiled, a glint of mischief in their eyes. "Let them talk. I'm not afraid anymore. We're stronger together, and I want the world to know it. Besides, I have your back, and you have mine."

Facing the World Together

Just then, they were interrupted by a familiar voice calling for Lucas. A teammate was looking for them, needing to discuss the post-match strategy. Lucas turned to Jamie, a flicker of uncertainty passing through their gaze. "This is it, isn't it? Time to go back into the spotlight."

"Yeah," Jamie replied, adrenaline coursing through them. "But we're going together this time. Whatever happens, we face it as a team."

As they walked back toward the group, Lucas reached for Jamie's hand, intertwining their fingers. The simple gesture felt monumental, a silent declaration of their commitment. They exchanged a reassuring glance, each gaining strength from the other.

The Announcement

Once they reached the team, the atmosphere buzzed with energy, players celebrating the victory and discussing their next steps. Lucas took a moment, gathering their thoughts, before addressing the gathered team and staff.

"Hey everyone, can I have your attention?" Lucas called, capturing the room's focus. The chatter faded, and all eyes were on them.

Jamie felt a flutter of nerves but also excitement. They sensed the weight of the moment, knowing what was coming.

"I want to take a moment to say something important," Lucas continued, their voice steady. "I know there's been a lot of speculation about my relationship with Jamie. I want you all to know that we are together. I love them, and I'm proud of that. No matter what the media says or what anyone thinks, we're in this together."

A Shared Response

Gasps filled the room, followed by a wave of supportive cheers and claps from teammates. Jamie felt tears prick at the corners of their eyes, a mixture of joy and relief flooding their heart. This was it—the public declaration they had both been so afraid to make.

Lucas turned to Jamie, their expression unwavering, as if inviting them to share in the moment. Jamie stepped forward, their heart racing but determined to stand firm.

"I love Lucas too," they said, voice clear and confident. "We're ready to face whatever comes next, together."

The applause grew louder, resonating with warmth and acceptance. The teammates rallied around them, offering support and camaraderie. Jamie felt the walls of doubt begin to crumble, replaced by a feeling of belonging and love.

Navigating the Aftermath

As the celebration continued, Lucas and Jamie exchanged glances filled with unspoken understanding. They had chosen each other, and that decision was stronger than any criticism or rumor that might arise.

Later, as the night unfolded and the team celebrated their victory, Jamie found a moment alone with Lucas again. "Are you really okay with this?" they asked softly, needing reassurance.

Lucas smiled, a genuine warmth spreading across their face. "More than okay. This is our chance to be real, to embrace what we have. I wouldn't trade it for anything."

Feeling emboldened, Jamie pulled Lucas close, their foreheads resting against each other. "Together, then."

"Always," Lucas replied, sealing their promise with another tender kiss, knowing that whatever challenges lay ahead, they would face them as partners, ready to tackle the world together.

Chapter 8: Finding Balance

Setting Ground Rules
In the quiet of Lucas's apartment, the tension from the world outside seemed to melt away. They sat together on the couch, the soft glow of a nearby lamp illuminating their faces. The thrill of their recent declaration still pulsed between them, but with it came the reality of their situation.

"We need to talk about how we're going to handle this," Lucas began, running a hand through their hair, their expression shifting from excitement to concern. "It's great that we're together, but we can't let the media dictate our lives."

Jamie nodded, feeling a mix of understanding and apprehension. "Right. I mean, we have to keep some things private to protect what we have. But how do we do that without hiding?"

Lucas took a moment to consider this. "Maybe we can establish some ground rules. Like, we can go out together but only in low-key places. Avoid the flashy spots where we're bound to be photographed."

"Good idea," Jamie replied. "And we should communicate. If something feels too much, we need to speak up. I don't want to lose what we have because of pressure from the outside."

Finding Common Ground
As they discussed their boundaries, the conversation naturally flowed into their respective careers. Jamie leaned back, thoughtful. "What about when it comes to games? I mean, we're rivals on the field, and that dynamic is tough enough without the added layer of our relationship."

Lucas met Jamie's gaze, appreciating the seriousness of the topic. "I think we can find a balance. It's about respecting our careers while also supporting each other. I'll always cheer for you on the pitch, and you'll do the same for me. But we can keep the personal stuff separate."

Jamie smiled, feeling relieved. "So, it's about keeping our professional lives intact while nurturing our relationship. I like that. We can be each other's safe space."

Moments of Connection

The conversation began to shift, the initial tension giving way to a playful energy. Lucas leaned closer, mischief in their eyes. "You know, we can make this work, but it might get a bit chaotic. Like, how do we deal with our fans when they spot us together?"

Jamie laughed, feeling a sense of ease wash over them. "I guess we'll have to get creative. We could come up with some fun ways to throw them off. Like wearing disguises or using code names."

Lucas chuckled, leaning back with an exaggerated expression of thoughtfulness. "Okay, how about this: you can be 'Captain Amazing,' and I'll be 'The Mystery Player.' That way, no one will suspect a thing."

"Perfect!" Jamie exclaimed, their laughter ringing through the room. "And if we get caught, we can just act like we're collaborating on some secret project for charity."

Building Trust

As the night deepened, the atmosphere shifted again, this time turning more serious. Lucas took a deep breath, looking at Jamie with sincerity. "But in all honesty, I want you to know that I trust you. This is new territory for both of us, and it's okay to be scared."

Jamie nodded, understanding the weight of those words. "I feel the same. I've never been in a relationship like this—especially with someone who's also in the public eye. But I believe in us. We can build a foundation based on trust and openness."

"Exactly," Lucas replied, their heart swelling with gratitude. "We'll face the challenges together. And if it gets overwhelming, we'll figure it out. We just have to remember why we started this in the first place."

Choosing Each Other

With that, they shared a quiet moment, the weight of the world around them fading into the background. The challenges they faced felt more manageable together, and a sense of hope blossomed within them.

After a beat, Jamie reached for Lucas's hand, intertwining their fingers. "So, what's our first step? I mean, how do we kick off this new chapter?"

Lucas grinned, feeling a rush of excitement. "Let's start small. We can schedule regular date nights, just the two of us. And if we ever feel overwhelmed by everything, we take a step back and have a chat—no judgment, just support."

Jamie's face lit up at the suggestion. "I love that. And maybe we can throw in some fun activities too—like practicing soccer tricks or even cooking together. Anything that feels normal."

"Normal sounds perfect," Lucas replied, their heart racing with anticipation. "Let's make our own normal, one day at a time."

Moving Forward

As they settled back into the comfortable silence, both players felt a renewed sense of purpose. Their relationship was not just about love; it was also about understanding, trust, and finding joy in the journey ahead.

With a shared resolve, they leaned into each other, the spark of a new beginning igniting between them. This was their moment, a chance to embrace both their love and their careers, navigating the complexities together and crafting a story uniquely theirs.

Game Day Anticipation

The stadium buzzed with excitement as fans filled the stands, their cheers echoing off the walls. Lucas stood on the sidelines, heart racing with a mix of nerves and excitement. Today was the day they would see Jamie in action after their recent commitment to openly support one another.

As the players warmed up, Lucas scanned the field, searching for that familiar figure. There he was—Jamie, focused and determined, moving with the grace and skill that had drawn so many eyes to him. The sight sent a surge of pride through Lucas.

Turning to a friend seated beside them, Lucas commented, "He's really on fire today, isn't he? Just look at the way he commands the ball."

"Yeah, he's impressive," the friend replied, glancing back at Jamie. "But you know the pressure's on him. This game could determine their chances for the playoffs."

Lucas nodded, feeling the weight of that truth. "I just hope he knows I'm here for him."

Moral Support on the Sidelines

As the match began, Lucas cheered loudly, joining the crowd in chanting Jamie's name. Every time Jamie touched the ball, Lucas felt a surge of adrenaline, their heart pounding with every play.

During a tense moment in the first half, Jamie made a bold move, weaving through defenders with ease. The crowd erupted, and Lucas felt a wave of pride wash over them. But when Jamie was tackled hard, a collective gasp echoed through the stands.

Lucas's stomach dropped as they watched Jamie hit the ground, pain etched across his face. They stood up, instinctively ready to rush onto the field, but they remembered their promise to each other: support from the sidelines.

As Jamie got back on his feet, brushing off the roughness of the tackle, Lucas couldn't help but shout, "You've got this! Keep going!"

Facing External Pressures

During halftime, Lucas spotted Jamie in the locker room, his brow furrowed as he spoke with his coach. They could see the tension on his face, a mixture of focus and the weight of expectations bearing down on him.

As the players made their way back onto the field, Lucas was there, standing at the sidelines, ready to offer a word of encouragement. When Jamie looked their way, they gave a thumbs-up and a reassuring smile. The tension in Jamie's shoulders eased, if only slightly.

After the game, which ended in a hard-fought win, Jamie ran toward the stands, his expression a blend of triumph and exhaustion. As he approached, Lucas met him halfway, throwing their arms around him in an embrace.

"Great game! You were amazing out there!" Lucas exclaimed, the thrill of victory coursing through them.

Jamie grinned, the stress of the match melting away in Lucas's presence. "Thanks! I was so focused on the game, but seeing you there made all the difference."

Sharing the Spotlight

In the post-game excitement, Lucas could sense the external pressures weighing on Jamie, especially from the media. Reporters gathered outside the locker room, eager to capture every moment, every expression.

"I'm not sure I'm ready for this," Jamie admitted, anxiety flickering in his eyes as he glanced toward the throng of reporters. "They're going to be all over me about today."

"Just be honest," Lucas encouraged. "You did great, and you've got me behind you. Let's face this together."

As they approached the media horde, Lucas squeezed Jamie's hand for reassurance. The cameras flashed, and reporters clamored for attention. Jamie took a deep breath, visibly steadying himself with Lucas by his side.

"Today was intense," Jamie began, his voice confident as he spoke to the reporters. "But I had my teammate and partner supporting me from the sidelines. That's what matters most."

Lucas felt a rush of warmth at the acknowledgment. It was a small step, but it felt monumental. They were not just supporting each other privately; they were facing the world together.

Balancing Act

Later that night, as they returned to Lucas's apartment, the excitement from the game still lingered in the air. Jamie plopped down on the couch, exhaustion washing over him.

"Today was overwhelming, but having you there made it bearable," he admitted, rubbing his temples.

"I wouldn't miss it for the world," Lucas replied, settling beside him. "But we need to keep talking about how to handle all this. It's one thing to support each other in private, but facing the world adds a new layer."

Jamie nodded, the reality settling in. "Yeah, we need to figure out how to maintain this balance. It's a lot to juggle."

"Together, we can handle it," Lucas reassured him, leaning in closer. "We just need to stay grounded in what we have. Our love can be our refuge from everything else."

Finding Strength in Each Other

As they sat in comfortable silence, Lucas felt the weight of the day's events begin to dissipate. They knew challenges lay ahead, but having each other's backs was a strong foundation.

Jamie turned to Lucas, a playful smile breaking through the fatigue. "So, what's the plan for our next game day? More disguises?"

"Absolutely!" Lucas laughed. "Maybe we'll even coordinate outfits. I could wear a jersey with a fake mustache."

"Perfect! Captain Amazing and The Mystery Player will keep the fans guessing!" Jamie teased, feeling lighter with each shared laugh.

With laughter echoing through the apartment, they began to envision their future, not just as athletes but as partners ready to take on whatever challenges came their way—together.

New Training Regimens

As the weeks rolled on, both players found themselves thriving in their respective games. Lucas and Jamie established a routine that seamlessly blended their training schedules with time spent together. They committed to pushing each other, not just in their personal lives but on the field as well.

One afternoon, they met at a local training facility, a quiet place where they could work without the prying eyes of the media. The air buzzed with anticipation as they warmed up together, playful banter punctuating their routine.

"Alright, let's see what you've got today," Jamie challenged, a mischievous grin on his face as he dribbled the ball effortlessly.

"Just watch and learn," Lucas shot back, determination lighting their eyes. "I've been practicing those footwork drills you showed me."

Pushing Each Other to New Heights

As they engaged in drills, Lucas felt the pressure of competition mixing with the excitement of working alongside Jamie. They practiced passing, shooting, and strategic plays, the intensity of their training fueling their growing skills.

"Nice shot!" Jamie praised, watching as Lucas landed a powerful strike on goal. "You're really improving. I think I might have some competition on the field."

Lucas laughed, their heart swelling with pride. "And you've been incredible too! I've noticed how you've refined your game. Your agility is off the charts."

Each compliment became a stepping stone in their relationship, a shared victory that deepened their connection. The more they trained together, the more they recognized how their love translated into performance.

Game Day Successes

As the season progressed, both players found themselves excelling in their respective teams. Lucas had developed a reputation for being a dynamic midfielder, while Jamie became known for his striking abilities. During games, they often caught each other's eye across the pitch, exchanging supportive nods and smiles.

After a particularly intense match where Lucas scored the winning goal, they celebrated with teammates, but their eyes quickly searched for Jamie in the crowd. Spotting him near the sidelines, Lucas rushed over, barely containing their excitement.

"You did it! I can't believe you won it for us!" Jamie exclaimed, pulling Lucas into a tight embrace.

"I wouldn't have done it without you pushing me every day," Lucas replied, breathless with exhilaration. "This is our victory!"

Acknowledging Their Journey

As the post-match celebrations began to wind down, the two found a quiet spot away from the noise of the festivities. Leaning against the cool metal railing of the stadium, Jamie turned serious.

"It's amazing how far we've both come. I never thought I could reach this level," he admitted, looking out at the field. "But having you by my side… it's made all the difference."

Lucas smiled, feeling a warmth spreading through them. "I feel the same. We've grown so much, both individually and together. I think our bond fuels our determination. It's like we can read each other's moves on the field."

Jamie nodded, a thoughtful expression on his face. "And it's not just the game. I've realized that having someone who believes in me has changed how I approach everything, on and off the field."

Celebrating Their Achievements

BREAKING THE RULES

As the season continued, they both received accolades for their performances, and their teams thrived. Friends and fans began to notice their growing synergy, often attributing their success to the newfound confidence they exhibited.

During an award ceremony, Lucas stood beside Jamie as they accepted a joint recognition for "Best Player Duo." The crowd cheered, and the moment felt surreal.

"This award isn't just about us; it's about the journey we've taken together," Lucas said into the microphone, looking at Jamie with a soft smile. "We've pushed each other, and through that, we've discovered our true potential."

Jamie added, "And it's proof that love can be a powerful motivator. Here's to more victories—together!"

Their heartfelt words resonated with the audience, and as they left the stage, they shared a knowing glance. The bond they forged not only strengthened their love but also their drive to keep improving.

Looking Toward the Future

Later that night, as they celebrated with friends, Lucas and Jamie found a moment alone. Lucas leaned against the balcony railing, gazing out at the city lights twinkling below.

"Can you believe how far we've come?" Lucas mused, a smile on their lips.

"It's just the beginning," Jamie replied, wrapping an arm around Lucas's shoulders. "Imagine what we can achieve if we keep this up."

Lucas turned to face him, their eyes sparkling with excitement. "Together, we can conquer anything—on and off the pitch."

As they stood there, the warmth of their connection enveloped them. They knew they were not just teammates; they were partners on a journey of growth, love, and endless possibilities.

Chapter 9: Trials and Triumphs

Injury Strikes

As the season progressed, the stakes grew higher. Lucas was in the midst of a crucial match when disaster struck. A reckless tackle from an opposing player sent them tumbling to the ground, pain radiating through their leg. The stadium fell silent as trainers rushed onto the field, and Jamie's heart dropped as he watched from the sidelines.

"Get up, you can do this!" Jamie shouted, desperation in his voice. But as the trainers helped Lucas off the field, he could see the grimace of pain etched on their face. The crowd's cheers faded into a dull roar as the reality of the injury sank in.

Later, in the locker room, Lucas sat on a bench, a towel draped over their shoulders. The team doctor delivered the news: a sprained ankle that would sideline them for several weeks.

"I can't believe this is happening," Lucas muttered, frustration bubbling beneath the surface. "This is the worst time for an injury."

Jamie entered the locker room, concern written all over his face. "Hey, it's going to be okay. We'll get through this together."

Team Conflicts

While Lucas was recuperating, tensions began to simmer within their team. The pressure of high expectations led to disagreements among players, particularly about tactics and leadership roles. Lucas felt the emotional toll, knowing they couldn't contribute to the discussions while injured.

One evening, as they sat at home, Lucas received a call from a teammate, expressing frustration about the mounting conflicts. "You need to be here, A. Things are falling apart without your voice. You always know how to bring the team together."

"I'm trying, but I'm sidelined," Lucas replied, feeling helpless. "I wish I could do more."

Jamie, who had been listening quietly, interjected, "You still have influence. You can support from the sidelines, and I'll make sure your ideas are heard."

Supporting Each Other Through Adversity

As the weeks passed, Jamie stepped up to fill the gap left by Lucas's absence. He took on more responsibility during practices and games, navigating the team dynamics with grace. But the strain of both supporting Lucas and managing the team weighed heavily on him.

One night, Jamie found Lucas sitting on the couch, deep in thought. "You okay?" he asked gently, sensing the weight of frustration hanging in the air.

"I just feel so useless," Lucas admitted, leaning back against the cushions. "I want to be out there with you, fighting for the team. Instead, I'm stuck here."

Jamie sat beside them, taking their hand. "You're not useless. Your strength isn't just on the field. You've taught me so much about resilience. We'll get through this, and when you're back, you'll lead us to victory."

The Road to Recovery

Determined to recover, Lucas committed to their rehabilitation. Jamie joined them during sessions, pushing them through exercises and providing encouragement. Their bond deepened as they navigated this challenging period together.

One day, while sweating through a workout, Lucas smiled, panting heavily. "I wouldn't be able to do this without you. You're my best coach."

"And you're my inspiration," Jamie replied, his gaze warm. "Watching you fight through this motivates me to give my all every day."

As Lucas gradually regained strength, they found a renewed sense of purpose. They began to brainstorm strategies and ideas for when they returned to the field, focusing on fostering team unity.

A Team in Crisis

Meanwhile, the conflicts within the team reached a boiling point during a critical game. Frustration erupted on the field, leading to heated arguments among players. Jamie, trying to maintain order, felt overwhelmed as tensions flared.

After the game, Jamie vented to Lucas over the phone, the sound of muffled cheers and shouts in the background. "It's chaos out here. We need you back to help fix this. I can't keep holding everything together."

"I wish I could just teleport to the field," Lucas replied, frustration lacing their tone. "Maybe I can arrange a team meeting. We can strategize on how to improve communication."

Jamie's voice brightened. "That's a great idea! I'll make sure everyone's on board. We can do this, together."

Overcoming Challenges Together

In the following days, Lucas reached out to teammates, sharing ideas and encouraging them to voice their concerns. They facilitated a meeting, despite being physically absent, and Jamie acted as the bridge, relaying Lucas's thoughts.

The team began to rebuild its cohesion, learning to communicate effectively. As tensions eased, Jamie noticed a shift in the atmosphere, a renewed spirit among the players.

When Lucas was finally cleared to return to training, the entire team celebrated. As they stepped back onto the field, Jamie greeted them with a broad smile. "Welcome back, superstar! Ready to lead us?"

"More than ever," Lucas replied, determination shining in their eyes. "Let's show them what we can do."

The Power of Unity

With Lucas back in the game, the team's dynamics shifted positively. They played with newfound unity and purpose, their bond fueling their performances. Together, they faced the trials of the season with resilience and determination.

As the final matches approached, Lucas and Jamie looked ahead with optimism. They had overcome personal challenges and team conflicts, proving that love and support could conquer adversity.

Standing together on the field before the last game of the season, Lucas turned to Jamie. "No matter what happens, we've faced so much together. I'm proud of us."

"Me too," Jamie replied, his hand finding Lucas's. "This is just the beginning."

As they stepped onto the pitch, ready to fight for their dreams, they knew they could weather any storm together.

Open Dialogue

As the weeks rolled on, Lucas and Jamie faced the reality of their demanding schedules. Balancing their burgeoning relationship with the pressures of the Premier League proved to be more challenging than either had anticipated. With injuries, media scrutiny, and team dynamics in constant flux, they realized they needed to communicate openly to navigate these trials together.

One evening, after a particularly grueling day of training, Jamie invited Lucas over for dinner. As they settled into the cozy atmosphere of Jamie's apartment, the tension of unspoken feelings hung in the air.

"Hey," Jamie started, nervously fiddling with the fork. "I feel like we haven't really talked about everything that's been going on. With the injuries, the team issues... it's a lot."

Lucas nodded, grateful for the opening. "Yeah, I've been feeling the pressure too. I think we need to be honest about how we're feeling, especially with everything we're facing."

Sharing Fears and Frustrations

As they dined, the conversation flowed from casual topics to deeper issues. Lucas shared their fear of not being able to contribute to the team, feeling like a burden while recovering from injury.

"I hate sitting on the sidelines. I feel like I'm letting everyone down, especially you," Lucas admitted, looking down at their plate.

Jamie reached across the table, placing a reassuring hand on Lucas's. "You're not letting anyone down. You're doing everything you can to support the team, and your presence means so much to us. I just wish I could help you more."

Lucas smiled, touched by the support. "It means a lot to me to hear that. I just don't want to drag you down with my struggles."

Creating Safe Spaces

After dinner, they moved to the living room, curling up on the couch with hot chocolate. The atmosphere was warm and inviting, perfect for deeper conversations. Jamie took a deep breath, ready to share their own struggles.

"I've been feeling the pressure too," he confessed. "With the media constantly watching us, I worry about how they'll twist our story. Sometimes, it feels like I have to put on a mask just to survive out there."

Lucas listened intently, recognizing the weight of Jamie's words. "You don't have to pretend with me. We're in this together, remember? Let's create a space where we can be honest about our feelings without judgment."

Jamie's eyes softened, grateful for Lucas's understanding. "You're right. I don't want to hide anything from you."

Setting Boundaries

As their relationship deepened, they also discussed boundaries and how to manage their public personas. Lucas expressed concerns about how the media often sensationalized their interactions, while Jamie worried about the potential impact on their careers.

"We need to figure out how to keep some aspects of our relationship private," Lucas suggested. "I want to protect what we have, but I also want to share it with the world."

Jamie nodded in agreement. "Let's find that balance. We can be supportive of each other without exposing everything to the public eye. Our relationship is ours to define."

Strengthening Their Bond

Over the next few weeks, Lucas and Jamie made a concerted effort to communicate more openly. They scheduled regular check-ins, where they could discuss their feelings, share updates on their training, and address any concerns without hesitation.

During these moments, they learned the importance of vulnerability, sharing not only their triumphs but also their fears and doubts. It became a safe space where they could express themselves fully.

One evening, after a successful training session, Lucas excitedly shared their progress. "I'm feeling stronger every day! I think I'll be back on the pitch soon."

"That's fantastic!" Jamie replied, beaming with pride. "And don't forget to take it easy. We want you at 100% when you return."

Celebrating Progress Together

As Lucas continued to heal, Jamie found himself thriving as well. Their communication fostered a supportive environment that empowered both of them to tackle challenges head-on. They celebrated each small victory together, recognizing how their love provided the foundation for their success.

On game day, Lucas attended the match, cheering passionately from the stands. Jamie spotted them as he scored a crucial goal, and their eyes met, filled with admiration and pride. In that moment, the support they had built through communication shone brightly.

After the match, Jamie rushed over to Lucas, pulling them into a tight embrace. "I couldn't have done it without your support. You're my rock!"

"I believe in you," Lucas replied, grinning from ear to ear. "Now, let's get ready for your next game!"

Looking Ahead

As the season continued, their commitment to open communication helped them navigate both personal and professional challenges. They became stronger not just as individuals but as partners, learning to trust each other more deeply with every conversation.

On a quiet evening, as they lay on the couch, Lucas turned to Jamie. "I'm so grateful for how far we've come. This relationship means everything to me."

"Me too," Jamie said, his voice sincere. "We've faced so much, and we're only getting stronger. Let's keep this communication going, no matter what happens."

As they held each other close, they knew that their journey would be filled with trials and triumphs, but with open hearts and honest conversations, they were ready to face whatever came their way.

Facing Challenges Together

As the season progressed, both Lucas and Jamie found themselves navigating a whirlwind of challenges that tested not only their skills on the pitch but also their relationship off it. Each trial they faced became an opportunity to grow closer, solidifying their commitment to one another.

The intensity of the Premier League brought fierce competition, with injuries and team conflicts looming large. Lucas, still in recovery, felt the frustration of not being able to contribute fully while their teammates battled for crucial victories. Meanwhile, Jamie grappled with the pressure of leading the team amid mounting expectations from fans and the media.

One evening, after a particularly tough match that resulted in a narrow loss, Jamie returned home exhausted. Finding Lucas waiting for him, he dropped onto the couch, burying his face in his hands.

"Another tough game?" Lucas asked gently, moving to sit beside him.

"Yeah, it's just... everything feels like it's falling apart," Jamie confessed, his voice muffled. "I don't know how to keep this team motivated when we keep losing."

Sharing the Load

Lucas placed a comforting hand on Jamie's back. "You're doing everything you can. You need to remember that it's a team effort. Let's focus on what you can control and support each other through this."

Looking up, Jamie met Lucas's gaze, feeling the warmth and understanding emanating from them. "I appreciate that. Sometimes, I just feel like I'm letting everyone down."

"You're not alone in this," Lucas reassured him. "We'll get through it together. Why don't we brainstorm some ideas to lift team morale? I may not be on the pitch, but I still have a few ideas."

BUILDING A SUPPORTIVE Environment

As they worked together, Lucas and Jamie found creative ways to connect and strengthen the team. They organized a team-building day, encouraging players to bond off the field, and Lucas contributed by leading a series of fun challenges and activities.

The day was a success, with laughter and camaraderie replacing the earlier tension. Watching Lucas engage the team with enthusiasm ignited a spark in Jamie. He realized how much Lucas's presence—whether on the pitch or off—elevated everyone around them.

"See? You've got this," Lucas said, grinning as they both watched the team compete in a friendly match of soccer tennis. "You're a great leader, and this team needs your energy."

Jamie smiled, feeling a renewed sense of hope. "Thanks for believing in me. I honestly don't know what I'd do without you."

Embracing Vulnerability

As the weeks passed, Lucas continued to support Jamie through the ups and downs of the season. They learned to embrace vulnerability in their relationship, sharing not only their triumphs but also their insecurities.

One night, after a successful training session, they sat on the balcony, overlooking the city lights. Lucas opened up about their lingering insecurities regarding their injury. "I've been worried that once I return, I won't be the same player I was. What if I let everyone down?"

Jamie took a moment to absorb their words, then said, "You won't. You're stronger than you think, and you've already shown incredible resilience. Just be yourself when you're back on the field. That's all anyone can ask for."

Tears prickled at Lucas's eyes. "Thank you for always reminding me of my worth. I've never had someone support me like this before."

"I'll always be here for you," Jamie replied, pulling Lucas closer. "We're a team, in every sense of the word."

CELEBRATING SMALL VICTORIES

As the season continued, the team gradually improved, and both players celebrated small victories. Lucas made significant progress in their recovery, and Jamie felt more confident in his role as a leader.

They began to carve out time to celebrate their achievements, whether it was treating themselves to a night out or simply enjoying a quiet evening at home together. Each shared moment brought them closer, reinforcing their commitment to each other.

One weekend, they decided to escape the pressures of the city, heading to a nearby cabin in the woods. As they hiked together, the beauty of nature surrounded them, providing a much-needed respite.

"This is exactly what we needed," Lucas said, taking a deep breath of the fresh air.

Jamie grinned, glancing at Lucas. "I couldn't agree more. Just being away from it all feels like a breath of fresh air."

As they reached a scenic overlook, Lucas turned to Jamie, eyes sparkling with gratitude. "I love how we can face anything together. No matter what challenges come our way, we always find a way through."

Strengthened Commitment

Returning from their getaway, they faced the upcoming matches with renewed determination. Lucas's recovery was progressing, and they were finally cleared to return to training full-time. The team welcomed them back with open arms, and the positive energy was palpable.

On the eve of a significant match, Jamie surprised Lucas with a small gift—a necklace with a charm representing their shared journey. "I wanted you to have something that reminds you of how far we've come together," he said, slipping it around Lucas's neck.

Lucas beamed, touched by the thoughtful gesture. "This means so much to me. Thank you for always being my rock."

"I'll always be here, no matter what," Jamie replied, a promise in his eyes.

As they held each other close, they knew that their relationship had deepened through every trial. Together, they had transformed challenges into stepping stones, solidifying their bond and commitment.

Looking Ahead

The next day, as they stepped onto the pitch together, both players felt a renewed sense of purpose. With their relationship strengthened by trials faced and triumphs celebrated, they were ready to tackle whatever lay ahead.

In that moment, they were not just teammates but partners bound by love, trust, and an unwavering commitment to each other. Together, they were unstoppable.

Chapter 10: Love Wins

The Championship Build-Up

The excitement in the air was palpable as the championship match approached. The city buzzed with anticipation, and the stadium was adorned with banners and fanfare. Lucas and Jamie had been preparing for this moment all season, their bond and teamwork having grown stronger through every trial they faced.

In the days leading up to the match, both players focused intensely on their training, determined to contribute to the team's success. Lucas, finally fully recovered from their injury, felt the adrenaline surge as they stepped back onto the pitch for the first time in the championship setting.

"Are you ready for this?" Jamie asked one evening during a final practice session, their eyes locked in a mix of excitement and nerves.

"More than ever," Lucas replied, a confident smile crossing their face. "Let's show them what we've got."

Game Day Tensions

On the day of the match, the stadium was filled to capacity, the cheers of fans echoing off the walls. As Lucas and Jamie took their positions on the field, a sense of unity and purpose enveloped them. They exchanged a quick, encouraging glance, a silent reminder of their commitment to each other and their team.

As the whistle blew, the game commenced with an electric intensity. The opposing team came out strong, testing the resolve of Lucas and Jamie. Both players showcased their unique styles, blending their strengths and instincts seamlessly. Lucas darted across the field with agility, while Jamie orchestrated plays with precision and leadership.

Midway through the first half, the tension escalated. The opposing team scored an early goal, sending shockwaves through the stadium. But instead of faltering, Lucas and Jamie rallied their teammates, refusing to let despair set in.

"We can turn this around!" Jamie shouted, gesturing for everyone to regroup. "Let's stick to our game plan!"

Pivotal Moments

As the match progressed, Lucas found themselves in a critical position. With only minutes left in the game, they received a pass from Jamie just outside the penalty box. Time seemed to slow as they calculated their move, the weight of the championship resting heavily on their shoulders.

"Trust yourself!" Jamie yelled from across the field, his voice cutting through the noise of the crowd. The reminder ignited a fire within Lucas.

With a deep breath, Lucas dribbled past a defender, then took aim at the goal. As they struck the ball, it soared through the air, the world around them fading away. The ball hit the back of the net with a satisfying thud, and the stadium erupted in a chorus of cheers.

Lucas's heart raced as they turned to celebrate, but their eyes quickly sought out Jamie. The moment their gazes met, a surge of joy and pride flowed between them. They had done this together.

A Dramatic Finish

With the score tied, the final minutes of the match were a whirlwind of energy. Both teams fought fiercely, every play filled with intensity. The clock ticked down, and Jamie found himself in a strategic position near the goal line, his teammates relying on him to create a scoring opportunity.

Lucas, sensing the urgency, moved to support Jamie. "I'm here!" they shouted, positioning themselves for a potential pass.

In a brilliant display of teamwork, Jamie managed to evade a defender and sent a perfect cross to Lucas. With the weight of the moment heavy on them, Lucas focused, their instincts taking over as they made the decisive play.

With a powerful shot, Lucas sent the ball flying into the goal, sealing their victory. The stadium erupted into euphoric cheers as teammates rushed to celebrate.

The Aftermath

As the final whistle blew, signaling the end of the match, the team erupted in jubilation. Lucas and Jamie found each other amidst the chaos, embracing tightly, hearts racing with triumph.

"We did it! We actually did it!" Lucas exclaimed, their voice muffled against Jamie's shoulder.

"Together," Jamie replied, pulling back to look into Lucas's eyes. "I knew we could. I believe in us."

In that moment, surrounded by the celebration of their teammates and fans, they knew their love had not only survived the trials but had flourished. They had each other, and together, they could face anything.

Love Wins

As the team celebrated their championship victory, Lucas and Jamie stood hand in hand, basking in the glow of their achievement. The triumph on the pitch was a reflection of their journey together—the trials, the misunderstandings, and the unwavering support that had brought them to this moment.

Amid the chaos, Jamie turned to Lucas, a soft smile on his face. "I don't want to just win titles with you; I want to build a life together. You've changed everything for me."

Lucas's heart swelled. "You've made me believe in love and partnership again. I want that too."

With the world around them fading into a blur, they leaned in, sharing a kiss that was both tender and passionate, a promise of a future filled with love, laughter, and shared dreams.

As they pulled away, the cheers of the crowd echoing in their ears, they knew that love had truly won. Together, they were unstoppable, ready to embrace whatever came next.

Post-Match Euphoria

The atmosphere in the stadium was electric. After a hard-fought championship match, Lucas and Jamie stood amidst a sea of ecstatic fans, confetti raining down around them. Their team had triumphed, and the adrenaline was still pumping through their veins. Amidst the celebration, they felt a surge of joy that was not just about winning the trophy, but about their journey together.

As teammates celebrated around them, Lucas glanced at Jamie, who was laughing and soaking in the moment. There was something different about today; the victory felt even sweeter, a reflection of their bond forged through trials and triumphs.

A Moment of Clarity

Jamie caught Lucas's eye and smiled, a knowing look passing between them. It was as if they both sensed that this was the perfect moment to embrace not only their victory but also their love. With the championship trophy glimmering in the background, Jamie took a deep breath, feeling a rush of courage.

"Can you believe we did it?" Jamie shouted over the noise, his eyes sparkling with excitement.

Lucas nodded, exhilaration coursing through them. "I couldn't have done it without you. This is our victory!"

As the team gathered for photos, Lucas pulled Jamie closer. "We should tell everyone how we feel. No more hiding," they whispered, heart racing at the thought.

Public Acknowledgment

When the time came for the trophy presentation, the team gathered at the center of the pitch, flanked by cheering fans and flashing cameras. The captain raised the trophy high, and the crowd erupted in cheers.

Jamie stood beside Lucas, his heart pounding with anticipation. As the captain finished his speech, Jamie felt an irresistible urge to seize the moment. He turned to the microphone.

"Before we wrap up, I just want to say something," he began, his voice steady but filled with emotion. The crowd hushed, curious about what he would say.

"I'm proud to be part of this team and grateful for our victory today," Jamie continued, looking out over the sea of fans. "But I also want to take this moment to acknowledge someone very special to me. Lucas has been my rock, my teammate, and… the love of my life."

Gasps echoed through the crowd, followed by a mix of cheers and surprised whispers. Lucas felt their heart soar as all eyes turned to them.

The Reaction

Lucas's breath caught in their throat, a mixture of disbelief and joy washing over them. They looked at Jamie, whose expression was filled with sincerity and love.

"I've spent too long worrying about what others think," Jamie said, glancing at the media representatives. "But I won't hide who I am anymore. Our love deserves to be celebrated, not whispered about in shadows."

The crowd erupted into applause, the surprise quickly turning into support. Fans began chanting their names, and the atmosphere transformed from one of shock to overwhelming love and acceptance.

Lucas stepped forward, taking the microphone from Jamie. "I couldn't agree more. We've faced challenges together, and today, I want to celebrate not just our victory on the field, but the love that has blossomed between us. It's real, it's beautiful, and it's worth sharing."

With that, the cheers grew louder, fans waving banners and chanting in support of the couple. Lucas and Jamie stood hand in hand, their hearts full, embracing the moment that would define not just their relationship, but their legacy in the sport.

A New Beginning

As the celebrations continued, the couple shared a passionate kiss, a symbol of their love that transcended the field. The press cameras flashed, capturing the moment that would forever be etched in history.

Later, as they made their way off the pitch, Lucas looked at Jamie with awe. "I can't believe we just did that. It feels incredible to be free."

Jamie smiled, squeezing Lucas's hand. "I knew we could face the world together. This is just the beginning for us."

Surrounded by the buzz of victory and the warmth of their fans' support, Lucas and Jamie walked side by side into their new future. They were no longer just teammates but partners, ready to tackle whatever challenges awaited them, united in love and triumph.

A Celebration Like No Other

With the championship trophy gleaming brightly under the stadium lights, Lucas and Jamie stood side by side, surrounded by their teammates and a roaring crowd. The thrill of victory coursed through them, but it was the knowledge of their shared love that truly made this moment unforgettable.

As they moved towards the locker room, laughter and excitement filled the air. Teammates congratulated them, high-fiving and cheering, but Lucas and Jamie shared a knowing glance that spoke volumes—today was about more than just the game; it was about their future together.

An Intimate Celebration

In the privacy of their locker room, the atmosphere shifted. The jubilant noise of their teammates faded as they found a quiet corner, away from the buzz. Lucas wrapped their arms around Jamie, pulling them close.

"I still can't believe we did it. We fought hard, and now we have this," Lucas said, gesturing to the trophy that symbolized their victory.

Jamie smiled, leaning in to place a soft kiss on Lucas's lips. "And we did it together. It's our win, not just for the team, but for us."

They celebrated, sharing stories of their journey, the obstacles they had overcome, and the moments that had brought them closer. With every word, their bond deepened, the foundation of their relationship solidifying in the warmth of shared dreams and ambitions.

Inspiring Their League

As the night unfolded, news of their public acknowledgment spread like wildfire through social media and the sports networks. They became a beacon of hope and inspiration for others in the league, showing that love could flourish even in the fiercely competitive world of professional sports.

In the days that followed, Lucas and Jamie attended interviews and events together, their confidence and joy infectious. They spoke openly about their journey, their love story serving as a powerful reminder that vulnerability and authenticity could break down barriers.

"You don't have to hide who you are," Jamie told a reporter during one interview. "Love should be celebrated, and it makes us stronger, not weaker. We want to inspire others to be true to themselves."

Facing the Future Together

As they prepared for the next season, Lucas and Jamie made a pact: to continue supporting each other both on and off the field. They began initiatives aimed at fostering inclusivity within the sport, speaking at events, and encouraging young athletes to embrace their identities.

In private moments, they shared dreams of the future—traveling together, possibly starting a family, and always making room for each other in their lives. Every day, they grew more committed to one another, facing challenges and celebrating successes as partners.

"I never imagined I could feel so free and so loved," Lucas admitted one evening as they watched the sunset from their apartment balcony.

"Me neither," Jamie replied, taking Lucas's hand. "We're just getting started, and I can't wait to see what's next for us."

With a sense of purpose and an unwavering bond, Lucas and Jamie stepped into a new beginning. Together, they were ready to face whatever the future held, knowing that their love would always guide them through the trials and triumphs ahead.

Also by Dow Jones

Breaking the Rules
Love's Dividends